Mills & Boon
Best Seller Romance

A chance to read and collect some of the best-loved novels from Mills & Boon—the world's largest publisher of romantic fiction.

Every month, six titles by favourite Mills & Boon authors will be re-published in the *Best Seller Romance* series.

A list of other titles in the *Best Seller Romance* series can be found at the end of this book.

Kay Thorpe

SUGAR CANE HARVEST

MILLS & BOON LIMITED
LONDON · TORONTO

All the characters in this book have no existence outside the imagination of the Author, and have no relation whatsoever to anyone bearing the same name or names. They are not even distantly inspired by any individual known or unknown to the Author, and all the incidents are pure invention.

The text of this publication or any part thereof may not be reproduced or transmitted in any form or by any means, electronic or mechanical, including photocopying, recording, storage in an information retrieval system, or otherwise, without the written permission of the publisher.

This book is sold subject to the condition that it shall not, by way of trade or otherwise, be lent, resold, hired out or otherwise circulated without the prior consent of the publisher in any form of binding or cover other than that in which it is published and without a similar condition including this condition being imposed on the subsequent purchaser.

First published 1975
Australian copyright 1983
Philippine copyright 1983
This edition 1983

© Kay Thorpe 1975

ISBN 0 263 74434 5

Set in Linotype Plantin 11 on 13 pt.
02–0983

Made and printed in Great Britain by
Richard Clay (The Chaucer Press) Ltd,
Bungay, Suffolk

CHAPTER ONE

THE WATER was warm and smooth like silk against Tessa's skin. She lay on her back gazing up at the great blue bowl of the sky, eyes slightly narrowed against the brilliance of the afternoon sunlight, limbs inert. Lethargy held her lightly in its undemanding grip, stretching the seconds to minutes and the minutes to infinity. Here in the still seclusion of the pool she might have been a thousand miles away from human habitation.

The plop of a pebble hitting the water close by her shoulder jerked her abruptly back to life. Putting her feet down to the tiled base, she shook a fist in mock anger at the tousle-headed boy standing grinning at her from the pool side, before striking out towards him. Her brother stood his ground as she lifted herself lithely over the edge, his eyes sparkling with eight years of accumulated mischief, the freckles bridging his snub nose standing out clearly against the pale chocolate of his skin. Oliver had been born right here in Barbados a couple of years after the Wright family had come out from England, and had never known any climate other than that of the West Indies. Eleven years older, Tessa could still recall bits from the old days, but felt no particular nostalgia. It was all too long ago and too far away. The island was home and she wanted no other.

'You'll be doing somebody an injury one of these

days,' she commented without rancour. 'Mom said you were to stop throwing things.'

'I didn't throw it, I tossed it,' came the ready retort. 'And I only hit something when I want to hit it.' He paused, hitching up the brief blue trunks around skinny hips. 'Mom's got a letter from America. Don't know who it's from, but she looked kind of funny when she was reading it.'

For his age Oliver's observation was pretty acute, Tessa reflected. Who could be writing to her mother from the States? They didn't know anybody over there. She finished squeezing out the worst of the moisture from her hair and ran experimental fingers through several thick strands, grimacing at the knots in it. It always finished up all tangled when she forgot to pin it up while she bathed, but it was too much trouble to mess about like that most of the time. More than once she had contemplated having the whole lot chopped off, but her mother was horrified by the whole idea. A lot of girls would give a fortune to have hair that shade without resorting to bleach, she was fond of saying. You should take pride in it. Tessa couldn't see what difference it made to the colour whether it was long or short, but to please her mother she left it as it was and continued to grumble every time she put a brush through it after a swim.

At nineteen Tessa was not unaware that most people seemed to consider her attractive to look at, but had not yet discovered any particular advantage in that fact. When she looked in a mirror it was strictly for functional purposes with eyes which took little note of the piquancy of her smoothly tanned features beneath the heavy sweep of honey-blonde hair. She wore dresses only when the occasion outlawed the jeans and shirt she normally preferred, and chose her closest friends from among those of her own age group who like herself were more interested in outdoor activities than dressing up for parties and other social functions. The only parties Tessa really enjoyed were the beach barbecues where everyone wore their oldest clothes rather than their best.

Having imparted his information in his own inimitable fashion, Oliver vanished once more into the shrubbery bordering the pool, intent upon some pursuit of his own. From where she stood Tessa could see through the arch of tropical evergreens across a wide stretch of lawn to the coral stone walls of the house, pink tinted behind sparkling white veranda rails. Things couldn't go on much longer like this, she supposed with regret. It was almost two months now since Waldron Marshall had died, and Bay Marris would hardly be allowed to stand empty for all time. Thinking of the man who had been like a second father during the three years since she had lost her own brought a pang. He had done so much for them, taking the whole family under his wing and throwing Bay Marris open to them at all times. He had been a true and very dear friend and they all missed him badly.

It seemed strange that Bryn Marshall hadn't bothered to visit his inheritance. He hadn't even attended the funeral, although to be fair there probably hadn't been time for him to reach the island before it took place: in this climate formalities were few and speedy in execution. Tessa supposed he was in touch with his uncle's solicitors, but so far there had been no indication of his intentions regarding the old plantation house itself. She hated the thought of seeing Bay Marris pass into a stranger's hands, yet even that would be preferable to having Bryn come back here to live himself. The five years since his last visit to the island had not in any way decreased her detestation. He would be thirty-one by now, but she doubted that he would have changed very much. People like Bryn Marshall didn't change. At least, not for the better.

With a faint sigh she slipped slim brown feet into raffia mules and headed in the direction of the boundary fence which separated the Wright property next door, leaving the moisture to dry on her skin as she walked. Colour danced before her eyes wherever she glanced, the brilliant red-orange of the flamboyant mingling with the delicate pinks and blues and yellows of oleander and hibiscus, the purple cascades of bougainvillea. At this time of the year the scent of frangipani dominated all others, sweet and tantalizing and emotive. Tessa broke off a small spray of the flowers, sniffing at it pleasurably as she twirled the stem between her fingers. The Barbadian spring was delicious, filling the trade winds with subtle fragrance. Caribbean spice time, her father had always called it.

Oliver Wright had been an author of some repute in the world of fiction, his novels likened to those of Somerset Maugham in their delineation of character and environment. They had earned him enough to bring his family out to a part of the world he had loved himself, and to keep them in fair comfort over the years until the sailing accident which had ended his life. Once or twice

Tessa had wondered idly how long it would be before his books stopped bringing in an income, but as her mother never showed any signs of worrying about the future she could only assume that provision had been made against that event. Meanwhile life went on as it always had, joyously carefree and full without being in the least bit demanding. Tessa could imagine no other way of living.

The sharp sting of a pebble on her bare thigh brought a yelp of pain to her lips. When she whipped round, Oliver was making off through the bushes towards the front of the house, his fair head catching the sunlight as he moved. So he only hit what he wanted to hit, did he? she thought wrathfully. Right, that made two of them!

Kicking off the encumbering mules, she took off after the agile figure of her brother, darting through the shrubbery with scant regard for bare limbs to see him already emerging on to the broad, tree-lined drive which swept up in a curve to the front steps. He was looking back at her and laughing, confident of his ability to outdistance her. The white, open-topped car which came whipping round the bend from the gates swerved violently to avoid the boy and screeched to a skidding stop with its front wheel bare inches from a tree, the gravel still dancing in its wake. Its driver let out a brief but succinct expletive and got out, viewing the long skid marks with grim mouth before turning his head to look at Oliver, who was frozen to the spot with shock.

'What's the idea of jumping out of the trees like that?' he demanded. 'You might have been killed, you young idiot! I've a damned good mind to tan some sense into you!'

Tessa came out of suspended animation and was halfway across the drive before she was fully aware of moving at all. Hands protectively on her brother's shoulders, she glared defiantly at the newcomer. 'Leave him alone! If you hadn't been going so fast you'd have seen him in plenty of time!'

Grey eyes held stormy blue for a long speculative moment before travelling slowly down over youthfully rounded curves to her slim bare legs, then back again to her face. 'Good grief,' he said, 'it's young Teresa all grown up!'

For the first time in her life Tessa became suddenly conscious of how little coverage a bikini afforded. Warmth swept up under her tan and she made a small involuntary movement which brought Oliver further round in front of her, the flush deepening at the leap of amusement in Bryn Marshall's eyes. It was like being fourteen all over again as she gazed up into the lean, clever features – at the mouth already pulling into the mocking smile she had so detested. His dark hair might be a little longer now, curling thickly into the nape of his neck, and he looked rather heavier in the shoulders beneath the immaculate tropical tan suit, but essentially he hadn't altered one iota from the last time she had seen him. He was certainly just as hateful. She made a valiant attempt to cover up her confusion.

'If we'd known you were coming today I'd have made sure not to trespass on your land,' she said with a swift lift of her chin. 'But you needn't worry, now that you are here we'll both stay off!'

If anything the amusement grew. 'Still the little spitfire,' he commented. 'I gather your mother didn't get my letter.'

That gave her pause. She looked at him with a faint line creasing her brow. Why would Bryn Marshall have taken the trouble to write to her mother after all this time? Apart from a brief letter of condolence at the time of her father's accident they had heard nothing of him since he had gone to England on the job which had helped put him where he was now.

'She had a letter today,' she admitted. 'From the States, I think.'

'That will be the one. I sent it over a week ago from New York. Trust it to be late arriving – although I don't suppose it matters over-much.' His glance went beyond her to the house, scanning its graceful lines with obvious satisfaction. 'It's good to be back. Pity it had to be in these circumstances, but that's life. I assume old Joshua is still looking after the place?'

'Yes.' Tessa bit back the question trembling on her lips. No doubt they would know soon enough what he had come back for. Meanwhile she had no intention of showing any interest whatsoever in his motives. 'You'll probably find him out back.' Her hand tightened a fraction on her brother's bony shoulder. 'Come on, Oliver.'

'There's no rush.' Bryn said it easily, one hand resting on the car door. 'You had the run of the place while Waldron was alive; there's no reason why you shouldn't continue to have it for the time being. Will your mother be at home after dinner if I call round?'

'I suppose so.' This time Tessa could not stop herself

from asking. 'What do you want to see her about?'

One dark brow lifted. 'Ever heard of social calls? Not all the Wright family shared your feelings about me five years ago, honeychild. I got on very well with your parents.' His expression altered a little, the line of his mouth softening. 'I was sorry to hear about your father. I had a great admiration for him.'

Something inside Tessa tautened abruptly and painfully. Three years had taken the edge off her loss, but she still couldn't talk about it easily – and especially not with *him*. 'I'll tell Mom you're here,' she said, and half turned to go.

Oliver shook himself free of her restraining hand and stayed where he was, looking up at the tall stranger with the bright light of curiosity in his eyes, his fright forgotten. 'Are you going to come and live here?' he demanded with a child's total lack of reticence. 'Tessa said you'd only be interested in making a profit out of a place like Bay Marris.'

'Did she indeed?' The words were soft, but the glance Bryn sent towards Tessa held a sudden glint. 'Well, your sister always did have very decided opinions on most subjects.' His smile lacked the mockery of a few moments before as he eyed the wiry young figure before him. 'You'll not remember it, but I used to ride you on my shoulders a few years ago. You were just a toddler then.' He inserted a certain inflection into his tone. 'No more dashing across the drive, old son. Next time you might not be so lucky.'

'Yes, okay.' There was no resentment in Oliver's ready agreement. 'It's a super car!'

'It very nearly wasn't,' with a glance at the tree

almost touching the front bumper. 'Behave yourself and I'll take you for a spin in it once I've got settled.' He opened the door and got back behind the wheel, starting the engine with a quick flick of his wrist. The lift of his hand in Tessa's direction held a taunt. 'See you later, honeychild.'

Tessa turned without a word and headed back into the shrubbery, leaving Oliver to follow at his own pace. She heard the car move on up the drive to come to rest again in front of the house and fade into final silence, and felt the quivering inside her begin to quieten a little. Bryn was back and nothing had changed. He still liked to tease and mock her, just as he had done in the past. Only this time he wasn't going to succeed in bothering her, no matter what he said or did. This time she would treat him with the indifference he deserved.

It took her several minutes to reach the point in the rear fence where Waldron had had a gateway cut through to allow the Wrights easy access to the estate. Beyond, the ground fell away a little towards the cane fields, edged by a row of majestic Royal palms tossing their green heads far into the sky. The sea was a deep blue line along the horizon, extending inwards towards the blur of white which was Holetown on the island's western coast. Out in the fields the cutters were still hard at work in the full gold light of late afternoon, arms rising and falling to a steady rhythm as they slashed at the waving stems reaching far above their heads. Snatches of pop music reached Tessa's ears as she angled down the slight slope towards her own home, bringing the whole scene back into the twentieth century with its transistorized overtones. A pity in one way, and yet she could never find it in herself to regret the passing of an age where the people at work down there would all have been owned like so many cattle by the rich planter who had built Bay Marris. She only hoped he had been one of the kinder, more charitable owners.

The Wright home lay beyond a hedge of scarlet bougainvillea, squatting comfortably in a slight hollow facing the sea. Tessa's father had designed the place to a simple plan which allowed for extension as and when required, adding on another bedroom when Oliver had been expected, and roofing in the veranda which ran along two sides of the single-storey building with wallaba shingles. The result was pleasing if not exactly luxurious. Tessa loved it even more than she loved Bay Marris. It was she who had christened it Greenways in reference to the twin lawns her father had cultivated with such tender care out at the front. A bit pretentious, he had always said, but he had painted the name on the board which swung at the entrance to the short drive under their own, heavily-branched tamarind tree. The fame of that tree with its rare 'sweet' fruit brought children from miles around to raid its branches when the fruit was ripe. And that wouldn't be long at all now, judging from the look of it.

She ran lightly up the three wooden steps and went in through the opened double glass doors to the large, multi-purpose living room. It was only when her bare toes came into contact with the cool pine of the interior floor that she remembered the sandals she had left in the shrubbery, but she had no intention of going all that way back to fetch them. They would be all right where they were until she went that way again – providing she ever did go that way again. It remained to be seen. While Bryn was in residence she doubted that she would be going anywhere near the house at all.

Shirley Wright looked up with a smile at her daughter's entrance, pushing aside the pile of mending she had been busying herself with and taking off the spectacles she wore only for close work. At forty-four she could quite easily have been taken for Tessa's elder sister rather than her mother. Only in certain lights did the tint of grey show up in the luxuriant brown hair which she wore cut short and curly the way Tessa would have liked her own, and that she steadfastly refused to do anything about. 'I'll take my lines and grey hairs as they come,' was her usual comment if the subject was ever mentioned.

'Did you see Oliver?' she asked now, rubbing the side of her nose where the glasses always marked. 'I sent him to look for you half an hour ago.'

'I saw him. He's on his way back – I think.' Tessa perched on the arm of the settee and regarded her parent with serious features. 'Bryn Marshall is here.'

'I know. At least, I knew he was due today.' There was the faintest of hesitations before her mother added, 'I had a letter from him saying he was coming, but it must have got delayed in the post. Have you spoken to him, or did you only see him arriving?'

Tessa said, 'He almost knocked Oliver down in the drive, and then had the nerve to threaten him. He's just as beastly as he ever was!'

Shirley's lips twitched. 'That would have been relief at having missed him. It's a natural reaction to feel like slapping a child when they've given you a scare.

Anyway, Bryn was never as bad as you made out. A bit of a tease, perhaps, but then you used to ask for it, following him around the way you did.'

Tessa went hot. 'I did *not* follow him around,' she said with as much dignity as she could muster. 'I couldn't stand the sight of him. I still can't.'

'All right, so you don't like him.' Her mother's tone was tolerant. 'It isn't important.' She paused. 'Val Wyman rang up a little while ago. They're having a party on Saturday night. Will you go?'

Tessa wrinkled her nose. 'All those stuffy business folk in best bibs and tuckers – no, thanks! Val knows I hate that sort of thing.'

'You could try making an occasional effort,' suggested her mother on a dry note. 'Val's a nice young man, and he seems to think rather a lot of you. Heaven only knows why he bothers after all the rebuffs you've given him.'

'I don't mind Val so much,' Tessa stated. 'It's just the kind of life he leads. All he thinks about is the business – like his father.'

An odd expression passed fleetingly across her mother's attractive features. 'To make a success of anything there has to be a certain amount of dedication. Roland made Wyman's one of Bridgetown's best and biggest stores through sheer hard drive and determination, and it's to his credit that Val shares his enthusiasm. Don't call him down just because he doesn't have time to indulge in your kind of pastimes. It would do one or two of your other friends good to put in a day's work now and then.'

'They do,' in quick defence. 'Blake Summers is off to

university this next term, and Rob is joining a team going up the Amazon by hovercraft next month.'

'I thought that had been done.'

She shrugged. 'It seems it's going to be done again. I think they're planning to explore one or two of the tributaries on this trip. Rob expects to be away about three months altogether. You can't call that sitting around being idle.'

'No, but I could think of more useful ways he could apply his energy.' Shirley shook her head resignedly. 'Anyway, I really think you might go to this party on Saturday, just for once. There'll be other young people there too. The Wyman parties are always a social draw.'

Tessa looked at her for a moment. 'Are you going?'

The reply was casual. 'I expect so. It isn't me we're discussing at the moment.'

'No.' On impulse Tessa bent down and planted a light kiss on her mother's cheek. 'If you really want me to go I will, providing I don't have to wear anything too got up.'

'At your age you can get away with anything,' Shirley smiled. 'I'll have a look at your yellow cotton. I seem to remember one of the straps hanging by a thread the last time I saw it. That should do perfectly.' Another pause, then she said on a different note, 'Did Bryn say anything about coming round at all?'

'Yes tonight.' Tessa selected a banana out of the bowl on the nearby table peeling it and taking a bite before adding 'I'll probably go out. Blake suggested going down to the beach for a moonlight swim.'

'Just you and him?'

'He didn't say. I shouldn't imagine so. He's calling round for me about seven.'

Her mother was frowning faintly. 'I'd rather you stayed round here, Tessa. No matter what you think of Bryn Marshall it's a bit impolite to be out on his first night here. In fact I was thinking of asking him over for a meal. I don't imagine Joshua will have got anything much in, and he'll be ready for a good dinner after travelling through from New York.'

'What was he doing in New York?' asked Tessa, momentarily sidetracked. 'I thought he was supposed to be working in South America.'

'That was months ago. He's been in the States since Christmas, apparently. Bridge-building goes on all over the world.' Shirley got to her feet with an air of decision. 'I'll give him a ring now and ask him.'

Tessa was dismayed. Having Bryn come over here at all would be bad enough, but to have to face him across the dinner table would be more than flesh and blood could stand. Yet she knew she wouldn't be able to get out of it now. It wasn't very often her mother used that particular tone, but when she did she really meant what she said, and Tessa wouldn't have dreamt of defying her. The moonlit swim would have to wait for another night, that was all, only it wouldn't help to think of the others enjoying themselves down on the beach while she was stuck up here being polite to their next-door neighbour.

Oliver arrived on the veranda carrying one of the tiny green lizards with which the island abounded in his cupped hand.

'This one's really tame,' he announced with enthusiasm. 'It's not even trying to get away.'

'It's probably scared out of its wits,' commented his sister. She finished off the banana in two huge bites and tossed the skin into the waste basket down by the side of the settee. 'Let the poor little thing go. How would you like to be clutched in a grubby fist?'

'It isn't dirty. Not very, anyway. I'm not hurting him. He's already getting to know my voice. Look . . .' He put his face down close to the creature and said 'Hallo, Lizzy,' at a volume which sent the lizard scurrying wildly up his arm to his shoulder where it clung in panic. 'See,' he said with pride, rescuing it from its precarious perch. 'I told you it was tame.'

'Put that thing down, Oliver,' ordered his mother, coming back into the room in time to catch the last words. 'I've got enough of your livestock around the house without bringing in any more.' She watched him reluctantly comply, then looked back to Tessa. 'Bryn's coming at eight. I thought you might feel like making one of those Creole fish casseroles to welcome him back to Bajan food. You're better at native dishes than I am.'

Tessa gave in. 'If you like. I could do a pineapple mousse for afters while I'm at it.'

'Lovely.' Her mother sat down to her mending again, pausing with glasses in hand to add, 'And Tessa, do put on a dress for once, will you? Maybe I'm too fussy, but I'd hate Bryn to think we didn't have any kind of standards left. You know your father always insisted on dressing properly for a meal.'

'Yes, I remember.' She said it softly. 'All right, Mom, I'll wear a dress.'

She went through to the white-walled hall, and from there across to her own bedroom with its cool green and white paper and louvred furnishings. The divan was spread with a pale green cover, on top of which sat the battered teddy bear Tessa had brought with her from England all those years ago. She called him Fred and wouldn't have parted with him for a fortune, despite the ribald remarks he had drawn at times from certain of her friends. She picked him up now and sat down with him on the bed, straightening the red bow about his scraggy neck with tender fingers. Dear old Fred, always here when she wanted comfort of any kind. She had sat and wept the first tears she had been able to cry into his fur on the day of her father's funeral.

If only her mother could meet someone really nice and get married again, she thought. She was still young and attractive enough to make another start, and it would be good for Oliver to have a father again. The trouble was that stuck out here they saw very few people on a regular basis, and since Waldron had gone there hadn't been nearly as many invitations. Tessa tried to imagine the kind of man she wouldn't mind accepting herself, and came to the conclusion that he would have to be very special indeed to step into her father's shoes. Offhand she could think of no one among the Wright circle of acquaintances who might fit the bill, which made the possibility remote unless someone new came on the scene.

Indirectly that brought her thoughts round to Bryn Marshall and the coming ordeal. For her mother's sake she was going to have to make an effort to be pleasant to him tonight – on the surface, at least. Providing he left her alone it wouldn't be too bad, she supposed, but she had a feeling that it wasn't going to be that easy after this afternoon's little episode.

The recollection of what her mother had said about the time he had been here before brought a curling sensation deep down inside her. It was true up to a point that she had followed the younger Bryn around. On first acquaintance she had thought him wonderful, and had quickly developed a crush which died even more swiftly on getting to know him better. What made it worse was that she knew he had been well aware of her feelings and hadn't cared a whit about hurting her. He was cruel and heartless, and she pitied anybody who made the mistake of getting involved with him. It was probably indicative of his attitude towards women generally that he wasn't yet married, although no doubt he had plenty of women friends. His type always did. She wished heartily that he had stayed away from Barbados altogether. No matter how much she tried to convince herself that he wasn't going to have any effect on her life she had a disquieting premonition of change already looming on the horizon. And not change for the better either.

CHAPTER TWO

DARKNESS came swiftly and softly stirring the crickets to vibrant life. At seven-thirty Tessa put on a short linen tunic in pale blue and tucked her hair back behind her ears with a loosely tied velvet ribbon. A touch of pale pink lipstick constituted her final concession to the demands of formality. Even had she possessed some it would never have occurred to her to use make-up on her face. All that gooey stuff wasn't for her. She liked to feel her skin fresh and clean after a shower, not clogged up with powder and cream.

Her mother nodded approval when she drifted back into the living-room. 'That's better. Now you look like a girl instead of an urchin. I sometimes think you ought to have been born a boy. It might have saved a lot of wear and tear in the long run.'

'I wouldn't have minded,' Tessa replied mildly. 'If I'd been a boy I could have gone off with Rob up the Amazon. They're not taking any females along. Rob says they're incapable of standing the pace. Typical male egotism! I'd love to be able to prove him wrong.'

'Well, you can't, thank goodness,' Shirley said with some impatience. 'Up the Amazon indeed! Did you let Blake know not to bother calling for you?'

'I left a message.' Tessa strolled to the open doors and stood looking out into the night, sniffing the familiar fragrance of jasmine and night-blooming cactus. The sky was clear, the stars bright enough to light up the landscape as far as the rise over which Bryn would probably come – unless he got out the car and came round by road. She listened to the cicadas, closing her eyes and leaning back against the jamb. It was a sound she never tired of, a sound she had never learned to take for granted like most who lived in these regions. The breeze wafting up from the coast played over her bare arms, deliciously cool and refreshing. She wished she could just go on standing here like this all evening instead of suffering what was to come. It was going to seem so awfully long and drawn out.

Bryn was at the foot of the steps before she realized he had arrived, pausing there to view her slender figure outlined against the light from within with a smile which brought her sharply upright. He was wearing a light linen suit in pale fawn which emphasized his breadth of shoulder while fitting snugly about narrow hips. Tessa felt an odd dryness come into her throat as she met the grey regard.

'Another surprise,' he said. 'I don't recall ever seeing you in anything but pants and shirts last time I was here, although I suppose five years has to make a difference.'

More than he knew, Tessa told herself tautly. With her mother's eyes on the two of them she forced herself to acknowledge his greeting, preceding him into the room and sinking into a chair without bothering to see him comfortably seated first.

'Would you like a drink before we eat, Bryn?' asked her mother when the initial exchange of news was over.

'I wouldn't mind.' With some deliberation his eyes

came round to where Tessa sat drumming her fingers against the chair arm. 'Can you make a Pina Colada? It's years since I tasted the Bajan version.'

Without a word Tessa got to her feet and went over to the small mahogany cabinet which housed the drinks, letting down the fall front with what she hoped was a confident air. She knew the basic ingredients of a Colada and had on occasion made them up for members of her own set, but whether that same mix would satisfy a man like Bryn Marshall was another matter altogether. She was conscious of him watching her as she measured out quantities and had to concentrate hard to stop her fingers from changing into thumbs. Damn him, she thought viciously. Why couldn't he just let her get on with it instead of sitting there with that smile on his face! He knew exactly what he was doing to her and it obviously amused him no end that he could make her nervous.

He took the tall glass from her with a murmured word of thanks when she took it across at last, raising it to his lips and tasting the contents. Tessa found herself waiting in some suspense for his verdict, and was almost ashamed of the small rush of gratification when he nodded his approval.

'Perhaps just a touch more grenadine,' he said, 'but otherwise perfect.' There was humour lurking in his eyes as he glanced up at her. 'Thanks for the trouble, Tessa. I appreciate it.'

'Don't mention it,' she retorted sweetly, and went back to pour the crême de menthe her mother had asked for, along with a tall glass of iced lime juice for herself.

'Not acquired the alcohol habit yet?' inquired their guest on a casual note. 'Good for you.'

'Perhaps I just didn't feel like it tonight.' Tessa took a long and deliberate swallow out of her glass and set it down. 'Excuse me while I see to the food. It shouldn't be long.'

She stayed out of the room as long as she reasonably could, making a pretence of putting the final touches to various side dishes already carefully arranged. Oliver had put himself to bed on orders at eight. Tessa took a peep into his room and found him already asleep. She envied him the privilege of escape from what promised to be an even longer evening than she had anticipated.

The moment she went back into the living room she sensed a change in the atmosphere: a kind of tension which had not been present before. There was an odd look in her mother's eyes, an expression Tessa couldn't define. When she glanced in Bryn's direction he was looking into his glass without any kind of expression at all on his face.

'Dinner's ready,' she announced into the silence, and saw the two of them share a glance almost of conspiracy as they came to their feet. What was going on Tessa couldn't even begin to guess, but she determined to find out. It was with some inner turbulence that she took her seat at the table. Bryn had only been in the house half an hour and already he was creating undercurrents in their lives. Just what was it he wanted coming here like this tonight? There had to be a special reason why he had bothered with them at all so soon after arriving at Bay Marris.

The meal seemed to last an age. Bryn ate well of everything and congratulated Tessa on her cooking. Afterwards he sat and smoked a cheroot while she made coffee and cleared away the dishes into the kitchen for Martha, their daily help, to wash up in the morning, chatted casually about island affairs for another forty minutes or so, and at ten o'clock took his leave on the plea of needing an early night – an excuse which Tessa for one accepted with a pinch of salt. She barely waited until he was out of earshot of the house before broaching the subject which had been consuming her for the last hour and a half.

'He said something to you earlier on, didn't he?' she asked with some urgency. 'Am I allowed to know what he was after?'

Her mother looked at her for a long moment before answering, the odd uncertainty back in her face. 'He made me an offer,' she said at last. 'A very good offer, Tessa.'

'An offer?' Tessa didn't understand immediately what she was getting at. 'For what?'

'This place – all of it.' Shirley added quickly, 'We wouldn't get anything like the same price on the open market. He's being more than generous.'

Tessa stared at her in blank astonishment and said the first thing that came into her head. 'What on earth would he want with Greenways when he already has Bay Marris?'

'Room to extend.' Shirley put out a hand and adjusted a small ornament a fraction of an inch. 'Apparently he intends to turn Bay Marris into one of those exclusive clubs, and wants our land for part of a golf course he plans to have laid out.'

'I knew it!' on a note of contemptuous triumph. 'I said from the first that he'd only be interested in what he could get out of it.' She paused, registering her mother's expression in dawning dismay. 'You're not actually considering selling to him, are you? You can't!'

The reply came with some reluctance. 'I'm not sure we can afford to turn down an offer like this one. With the kind of money Bryn is willing to pay we'd be able to do all sorts of things. We could even take a trip back to England. I'd like to see my few remaining relatives again.'

'I don't want to go to England!' Tessa couldn't believe what she was hearing. Leave Barbados! She looked at her mother in wide-eyed appeal. 'You don't really mean it? You wouldn't really sell Greenways to *him*, would you?'

A mingling of exasperation and some other less obvious emotion passed across the other's face. 'Don't talk about him like that. I'm tired of this attitude of yours to a man who's done nothing to deserve it.' She stopped, made a sudden weary little gesture. 'Let's leave it for tonight. It wasn't a good time to start discussing it in the first place. We'll talk about it tomorrow when we've both had a good night's sleep.'

It was no use arguing when she spoke in that particular flat tone; Tessa knew better than to even bother trying. She said goodnight through stiff lips and went to her room, sinking on to the bed in a kind of stunned misery which gradually gave way to a desire to wreak vengeance on the source of all the trouble. She had been right about Bryn causing an upheaval in their lives. Not content with inheriting an estate like Bay Marris, he was even trying to take their measly acreage as well! But he wasn't going to get away with it. Not without a fight. He might have got her mother half persuaded, but he was going to find out that the battle was by no means won. In fact she would go and tell him so herself – right now – tonight. Nothing like striking while the iron was hot, and hers was at melting point!

The house was quiet as she crept across the darkened living-room and let herself out by the veranda doors. It was still only just after ten-thirty, and with the moon up there was no difficulty in seeing her way. There was a light on in the kitchen premises when she emerged from the cluster of trees which backed the rear lawns. Without stopping to think about it, Tessa ran up the short flight of stone steps from the basement area and into the modern, blue and white tiled kitchen, startling the elderly Bajan already occupying it almost out of his skin.

'Hey, Miss Tessa, yuh mos' had me limbless bustin' in that way!' he greeted her reproachfully. 'What yuh wantin' this time of night?'

'Sorry, Josh.' In the bright light of the kitchen Tessa felt her resolve falter a fraction and made a conscious effort to gloss over that momentary weakness. 'I want to see Mr. Marshall. Is he still up?'

He looked surprised. 'Was in library las' time ah seen he.'

'Thanks, Josh, I'll find him.'

She passed across the kitchen to the far door, and along the symmetrical green and white tiled floor to the inner hallway, for once failing to admire the perfection of Waldron's taste in decor. The library door was closed, but nothing was going to stop her now, having got this far. Mouth set tight, she turned the knob without bothering to knock and stormed into the room, fixing the man who looked up from the huge mahogany desk under the curtained window with a blazing blue glare.

'I suppose you think you've got everything cut and dried,' she burst out. 'Well, you can think again, *Mr.* Marshall! You won't get Greenways at any price!'

Without moving from his seat Bryn said quietly, 'Close the door, Tessa, and calm down.'

She closed the door, taking satisfaction in doing it hard. Seeing him sitting there so unconcernedly with a cheroot in his fingers added fresh fuel to the fire, blanking her mind to everything but the need to put across her opinion of him in a way he couldn't fail to comprehend.

'People don't matter to you, do they?' she shot at him. 'They never did! All you care about is making money. Your uncle spent ten years restoring this house and grounds for pleasure, not profit, but you wouldn't be content to just live in it. Oh no! *You* have to make it into a paying proposition – and if anyone stands in the way they can always be bought out. Well, you're not doing that with us. I won't let you! I'll see you . . .'

'I think that's enough for the moment.' Jaw set hard, Bryn crushed the remains of the cheroot into a glass tray and got to his feet. He had taken off his suit jacket and was minus his tie, the open neckline of his pale cream shirt revealing a triangle of dark hair below the brown column of his throat. He looked big and powerful and, right at this moment, dangerous. Tessa swallowed a little, but refused to give way to the stirring of apprehension deep down inside her. He didn't frighten her. Everything she had said was the truth, and he couldn't deny it. She stood her ground, fists clenched at her sides as he moved out from behind the desk.

'Sit down,' he said, indicating a chintz-covered armchair set at right angles to the packed shelves of books lining the whole of one wall. 'And get a hold on yourself.'

'I don't want to sit down, thanks.'

'You'd better.' He still hadn't raised his voice, but there was no mistaking the impatience in his tone.

Tessa's head lifted. 'I'm not a kid now. You can't order me around like you used to. It's time someone told you where you got off!'

'I agree you don't *look* a kid any more,' Bryn's lips twisted sardonically, 'but underneath you're still the same little hothead. It's about time you gained some sense. How did you think bursting in here like this was going to impress me?'

'I don't want to impress you.' To her horror she heard her voice tremble on the last word; she made an effort to control it. 'I don't want anything to do with you. The only thing I came for was to tell you you were wasting your time trying to buy Greenways.'

'Isn't that up to your mother to decide?' He leaned against a corner of the desk, pushing his hands into his trouser pockets and studying her with a gleam of derision. 'That land belongs to her, not to you, and she certainly didn't turn down my offer out of hand. You've obviously talked about it with her. What exactly did she say?'

Tessa drew in a shaky breath. 'Oh, I don't deny you

tempted her. You'd make sure of that, wouldn't you? But Mom loves Greenways just as much as I do, and she's never even thought about leaving before this. Once she's had time to think it over she'll say no quick enough, don't you worry.'

'You mean once you've given her reason to know how much you're against it,' on a hard note. 'You used to be very good at getting your own way with your father, but you might find your mother a different proposition when it comes to something like this. She's as strong-willed as you are.'

Tessa blazed, 'Leave my father out of it!'

'Unfortunately you're making that impossible.' Bryn paused, added with emphasis, 'Are you going to sit down, Tessa, because I am not prepared to discuss this any further with you standing there like a little virago.'

'There's nothing to discuss.' She could no longer conceal the tremor in her voice and didn't care. 'I've said all I've come to say, so I'll be getting back.'

'Not yet you won't.' He was across the room before she could move, taking her firmly by the upper arm and pressing her down into the chair he had indicated. 'You're going to sit there and listen to a few home truths before you get out of here.' His fingers tightened painfully for a brief few seconds at her attempt to resist him. 'You move or open your mouth again before I've finished and you're going to be sorry. You've had your say, now it's my turn.'

Tessa subsided abruptly. Bryn was treating her like a child still, being as hateful as only he knew how. She wished she had the nerve to defy him, but at the moment it was beyond her. She should have known better than to come here at all, she thought with bitterness. He had already proved himself singularly lacking in sensitivity.

'That's better.' He moved away, but only as far as the chair opposite, sitting on the arm to regard her with an expression which made her squirm inwardly. 'Did it occur to you that your mother might need to sell Greenways anyway?' he asked. He held up a hand as her head came up. 'No, obviously it didn't. Any more than you ever probably gave a thought to anything beyond what Teresa Wright wants out of life.' He paused, his mouth taking on a new slant. 'For your information, honey, three people can't live on fresh air – and that's all there's going to be soon if something isn't done. Your father's novels were good, but he only wrote one a year, and even then I understand his sales never quite lived up to his reviews. Just how long did you think they'd go on bringing in an income adequate to your expenses as a family? It's been three years, Tessa, and apparently his publishers aren't planning any more reprints. If it hadn't been for a small life policy he left you'd have been looking for a buyer for the house some time ago.'

Tessa sat in stunned silence for several seconds after he had finished speaking. It wasn't true! It couldn't be true! But she knew it was. Not even Bryn would make up a story like that.

'You only spent about fifteen minutes alone with Mom tonight,' she said at last. 'She couldn't have told you all this in that time.'

'No, she didn't. Waldron told me some of it in his letters, the rest I pieced together for myself.'

Her eyes were dark. 'He had no right to discuss our affairs with you! If my mother shared her worries with him she would have expected him to keep them to himself.'

'She didn't have to share them. Waldron was an executor in your father's will. He knew the circumstances without being told. He wanted to help, but he also knew your mother would never accept any kind of financial aid without doing something for it, so he hit on the idea of turning Bay Marris into a country club and incorporating your land with his.' He paused. 'He planned to offer your mother a job and have the three of you move in here to help run the place eventually.'

Tessa stared at him, her throat tight and aching. 'He was going to do all that just for us?'

A smile touched Bryn's lips faintly. 'Oh, I daresay he had an eye open to business too. He'd been contemplating either selling the place or doing something constructive with it for some time before he got hold of this idea. It was far too big for one man. Basically I thought the idea a good one.'

'Except for the part about having us here to live with him,' Tessa surmised on a sudden flash of intuition. 'You didn't think much to that, did you?'

He shrugged. 'I didn't think it would work out under the circumstances. It might have been different if he'd been prepared to ask your mother to marry him.'

'Marry!' Astonishment widened her eyes. 'But...'

'Oh, a man of sixty isn't past feeling emotion.' Bryn's tone was dry. 'Waldron was in love with your mother for years – even when your father was alive. I guessed that much when I was here five years ago. The trouble was he'd convinced himself that he was too old for her, and that he'd ruin everything by suggesting a closer relationship. The job was going to be by way of a compromise. That was why I didn't believe it would work.'

Tessa could appreciate that latter statement. The word compromise would not figure largely in Bryn Marshall's vocabulary. For him it would always have to be all or nothing. She tried to assimilate what he had just told her, to imagine the Waldron she had known as a man capable of the depth of love he must have felt for her mother to have contemplated having her so near and yet so far. Looking back, she could think of times when he had perhaps revealed rather more than just a friendly interest — like the day last year when her mother had had the accident in the car and been taken to hospital. She could see Waldron's face now when she had gone to him for help in getting into town, white and strained — remember the relief in it when they had found the patient badly shaken up and slightly concussed but otherwise safe. She had thought little of it at the time, accepting his concern as natural to the nature of their association with him, but in the light of this fresh knowledge she could imagine what he must have gone through.

'Why did he never say anything?' she murmured, almost to herself. 'Why didn't he tell her?'

Bryn was watching her face. 'You think he might have stood a chance of having his feelings returned?'

Tessa considered the question for a moment, then shook her head confusedly. 'I don't know. Mom thought an awful lot of him, but I'm not sure if it went any deeper than that.'

'Well, it's something to have *you* uncertain for once. Anyway, it hardly has much bearing on the situation at present. I only passed it on to clear up any misunderstandings in your mind as to his motives.'

'It still doesn't excuse him passing on private affairs to you,' she came back hardily. 'You had no interest in us as a family. Why should it be any concern of yours?'

The grey eyes sparked briefly. 'Who says I had no interest? I knew all of you, and Waldron had no one else to talk things over with.'

'It's a pity then that you didn't visit him a bit oftener.' It was out before she thought about it, although she wasn't sure she would have kept it back in any case. She saw his face harden again, and thought recklessly that she might as well be hanged for a sheep as for a lamb. 'Of course, you were far too busy getting to the top to bother about an old man's troubles – until he came up with an interesting business proposition, that is. Now that it's all yours you can even cut out the bits you didn't like about the idea. Take Greenways over, sure, but to hell with the Wright family!' The words were coming thick and fast, spilling from her with all the pent-up resentment of five years. 'So far as you're concerned the sooner we're out of sight the better. Isn't that about right? You couldn't even wait until tomorrow to come round and start the ball rolling. I'm only surprised it took you as long as it did to get here. Just think of all that wasted time!'

Bryn was sitting very still, looking at her as if he'd never really seen her before, the skin around his mouth showing white beneath the tan. 'Finished?' he inquired softly as her voice petered out. 'Or would you like to add a rider or two while you have the chance?'

Tessa was silent, her heart thudding against her ribs. She had gone too far; he didn't need to say it, she knew it. Regardless of how she felt about him, what she had said was unforgivable. She wanted to apologize but didn't know how to start. In any case, she doubted that she would be allowed to. From the way Bryn looked he wasn't in any mood to listen to anything further from her.

She was right about that. He rose abruptly to his feet. 'I think it's about time you went home,' he said. 'I'll see you through the top gate.'

She said thickly, 'You don't need to do that.'

'Maybe not, but I'm going to.' There was an inflexible line to his jaw. 'I'm not entering into any further arguments. I just want you out of the house. Now!'

Tessa rose without a word and walked out of the room, conscious of him close behind her. They went out the way she had come in. She was glad to find Joshua gone from the kitchen. The old manservant had known her too long not to have realized that something was wrong.

Bryn made no attempt to talk as they made their way through the rear gardens to the boundary fence. In the moonlight he looked cold and remote. Tessa felt the heaviness inside her like a dead weight. Coming up here had been a rotten idea. All it had achieved was to turn derision to contempt, and that she liked even less. Perhaps if she had waited and approached Bryn in a calmer frame of mind he might have been prepared to help her find some other solution to the problem. For all she knew he didn't really need Greenways at all but was simply carrying out at least a part of the plan his uncle had formulated to help them out of difficulties. Maybe it still wasn't too late. It would be humiliating to climb down after all she had said, but if that was what was needed . . .

Bryn opened the gate in the boundary fence for her, and paused. 'I'll watch you down the slope from here,' he said evenly. 'Good night.'

Tessa turned and faced him, gathering her courage to meet his gaze. 'Bryn, won't you let me . . .' she began, and felt her voice peter out before the look in his eyes.

'You never did know when to leave well alone, did you?' he said. 'I've taken as much as I'm going to take from you, Tessa, for tonight. My offer stands. That's it.'

Anger swept over her like a rip tide, drowning all desire to placate him. 'Then go to hell!' she choked, and ran off down the slope towards her own home as if the devil himself were hot on her heels.

In all Tessa's years on the island no night had ever seemed as long. Morning found her heavy-eyed and weary but resolved to carry on the fight regardless. Her mother was already having breakfast out on the veranda when she wandered through. She also looked as if she hadn't spent a very restful night.

'I wish you'd wear something on your feet round the house,' she commented resignedly. 'Really, Tessa, it's time you began taking some kind of pride in your appearance.'

'There doesn't seem much point at this time of the

morning,' the latter replied, slipping into a chair. 'Where's Oliver?'

'Over at Bay Marris, I expect. I caught a glimpse of him going over the hill when I came out here. You might go and have a scout round for him after you've eaten. I don't want him late for the school bus again.'

Tessa kept her eyes on her fruit juice. The last thing she wanted was to go anywhere near Bay Marris while there was any danger of meeting Bryn. Bother Oliver! Why couldn't he stay round Greenways now that the house next door was no longer empty?

'Have you thought any more about selling?' she asked, unable to bear putting off the subject any longer.

Shirley gave a small sigh. 'Yes, I have. It's all I've thought about all night.' She hesitated, looking across at her daughter with the indecision plain in her eyes. 'Tessa, perhaps it's too good an offer to turn down no matter what. Things . . . Things are starting to get a bit tight where money is concerned, I'm afraid. Having no regular income doesn't exactly help. I just can't count on what your father's royalties are going to be these days.'

'If a regular income is all we need I can get a job,' Tessa said eagerly.

Her mother smiled a little. 'Doing what? You're not trained for anything.'

'Val would help there. You know he would.' Tessa was leaning forward with her elbows planted on the table, intent on getting across how much consideration she had given this idea. 'Working for Wyman's I'd be bringing in a tidy sum — they pay very good salaries.

Enough to keep the three of us, at any rate.'

'*And* run a car and such other necessary little items?' The words were gentle. 'Tessa, I know you mean well, but...'

'It *could* work.' The blue eyes were pleading. 'Please, Mom, at least let me ask Val about it. It may not be a long-term solution, but it would help out, and something else might turn up before Dad's royalties fade out altogether.'

Her mother's expression was wry. 'Like a miracle, for instance. Did you have anything in particular in mind?'

'Well...' Tessa didn't look at her... 'you might even get married again. You're not all that old.'

'Thanks.' There was a curious quality in the gaze Shirley Wright bent upon her daughter's bright head. 'You mean you wouldn't mind?'

The head lifted. 'Not if it was someone you really wanted to marry. I mean, someone really nice and kind and...'

'And preferably rich?' Her mother laughed and shook her head. 'There's more to getting married again than considering the kind of man who would be suitable. There's such a thing as being asked, in the first place.' With some deliberation she changed the subject. 'Were you really serious about this job, Tessa?'

'Of course. I still am.' Her eyes brightened. 'Does that mean you'll agree to let me try?'

The pause was brief. 'It means,' Shirley said slowly, 'that I agree to your asking Val about the prospects of a job. If he says they might have some opening for you then I think we ought to discuss it with his father before coming to any final decision. After all, Roland might not care for the idea.'

Tessa couldn't see why not, but having got this far she was prepared to let it go at that for the time being. Saturday was almost a week away yet. She put the last piece of toast in her mouth, chewed and swallowed and said in as casual a tone as she could manage, 'What will you tell Bryn?'

'That depends when I see him again. He said he'd leave it a few days for me to think over.' Her mother rose and began clearing away the breakfast dishes. 'Martha will be here any minute. If you've finished, how about finding Oliver for me?'

With some reluctance Tessa got up. 'All right.'

She avoided going too near the house, cutting down through the shrubbery towards the pool, in the vicinity of which her brother was usually to be found. There was no danger of an accident there. Oliver could swim like a fish and stay under water for a full minute. Tessa never imagined him to be in very much danger anywhere around Bay Marris – fast driven cars excluded. She had seen him fall out of a tree and get up totally unconcerned. He was like a rubber ball, full of bounce, only that didn't stop her mother from worrying about him when he was too long away from home.

He was at the pool all right, but he wasn't alone. Tessa stopped within the shelter of the screening bushes and watched the man in the water swimming with strong even strokes towards the far end where the boy awaited him. Bryn said something as he hoisted himself out over the edge, but they were too far away for Tessa to hear. He stood with his back to her, the broad shoulders glistening with water in the sunlight, tapering down to a narrow waist and hips hugged closely by a pair of brief white trunks. His legs were straight and strongly muscled and not too hairy – Tessa disliked hairy men. She was aware of a churning sensation in the pit of her stomach, similar yet somehow different from the emotions he had aroused in her all those years ago. She wanted to move away, but she couldn't take her eyes off the tall, powerful figure of the man who was trying to ruin her whole life. It was like being held there by a magnet.

Oliver must have spotted her among the bushes, and said something, for Bryn suddenly turned and looked straight at her. It was too late then to think about getting away without a confrontation. Tessa steeled herself, and moved out into clear view as though she had only paused on the way.

'I came to find Oliver,' she said across the length of the pool. 'Mother was worried about him.'

'Of course.' Bryn's tone was pleasant enough, and there was certainly no indication of last night's anger in his expression – at least not at this distance. 'I'd just promised him a share of my English-style breakfast. I don't suppose you'd be interested in bacon and eggs yourself?'

Tessa fought the crazy impulse to say she would and treated him to a cool blue regard. 'I don't think so, thanks. Oliver, you'd better come now. You have to get ready for school.'

Bryn took a glance at the boy's crestfallen face and said, 'There's time enough if I send him right back after we've eaten.'

Tessa hesitated, recognizing the truth in what he said but reluctant to concede him even that much of a victory. 'He shouldn't have come in the first place,' she prevaricated. 'Not without telling one of us where he was going.'

Bryn moved impatiently. 'You knew darn well where he was coming. It was only yesterday that I told you both to go on using the place as usual.' He studied her for a moment, lips faintly mocking. 'The trouble with you, young Tess, is you don't take me seriously enough. I'll have to do something about that. Are you coming or going? Make up your mind.'

Seething, but outwardly in possession of herself, she said, 'I'm going. Oliver, you're to come straight home after breakfast.'

Her brother stuck his tongue out at her, then gave a muffled yelp as a hand took him by the scruff of the neck and shook him like a young puppy.

'Don't do that to your sister,' Bryn admonished him without raising his voice. He let the boy go, ruffling his hair as he looked back to where Tessa still stood. 'I'm going into Bridgetown this morning. Ask your mother if she needs anything, will you?'

He lifted a casual hand and went off towards the house, Oliver trotting at his side. Tessa bit her lip, conscious of having lost that round without being able to quite work out why. It was impossible to get the better of Bryn in an open clash, she acknowledged. He had proved that much last night. So why keep on trying?

She couldn't answer that question either.

Shirley received the news of Oliver's whereabouts resignedly. 'I hope he isn't going to make himself a nuisance,' she murmured.

Tessa shrugged. 'I'm sure Bryn will soon turn him out if he does.' She caught her mother's eye and added swiftly, 'I was thinking of running down into town for one or two things. Is there anything you want fetching?'

She hadn't actually meant to say that, she thought in some confusion. But it wasn't a bad idea now she considered it. There were a few items she needed, and it would make a change. If she got ready right away she would be there for nine, and probably out again long before Bryn reached town. Not that it made any difference, she told herself hastily. Bridgetown wasn't all that big, but it was unlikely that she would meet up with him.

Her mother accepted the offer in faint surprise, but she was too long used to her daughter's sudden whims to make any comment. Tessa went and changed into a slim-fitting linen suit the colour of thick cream, causing more lifted eyebrows when she went back to the living-room to get the car keys.

'Things *are* looking up,' her mother remarked with approval. 'Time was when you'd have been quite happy to go into town in a pair of jeans.' Her gaze rested a thoughtful moment on Tessa's face. 'It wouldn't have anything to do with our next-door neighbour, by any chance?' she asked lightly.

Tessa looked quickly away. 'Why on earth should it? I just thought I'd better start smartening myself up if I'm going after a job, that's all. You're always telling me I look like a street urchin.'

'Too true.' Shirley was smiling. 'Glad to see it's begun

to get through at last. You look good in that suit. You can't have worn it more than twice.'

Tessa grinned, and went over to press a swift kiss on her forehead. 'I'll try to keep it up. 'Bye, Mom. See you at lunch.'

It was hot in the little Morris. Tessa drove with the windows wide open, feeling the wind lifting her hair at her temples. A blue haze still clung to the hills in the Scotland district, giving way slowly to the rising temperature. Ahead lay the colourful, cultivated fields of sugar cane, yams and sweet potatoes, broken every so often by shallow gullies overflowing with lush tropical vegetation. Every bend brought a glimpse of the sea, unbelievably blue and placid on this south-westerly side of the island, the atmosphere so clear that even from here it was possible to pick out individual palms curving about a crescent of white beach.

Recalling her mother's brief mention of going back to England for a visit, Tessa felt a small pang of guilt. It was different for her, of course. She had grown up in England; she still thought of it as home. So far as Tessa was concerned it was just a place she had once lived in, and that was all. She didn't want to go back even fleetingly, although perhaps a part of the reluctance was the fear that somehow she would be forced into staying there for good. Anyway, the question didn't arise unless they were eventually forced to sell the house. And if they were, she vowed fiercely, she would make sure that it wasn't to Bryn Marshall!

Bridgetown was as busy as it always was, despite the comparative earliness of the hour. Tessa parked the car on the space adjoining the Careenage, and walked back along the Wharf toward Trafalgar Square, revelling in the scene of activity, with inter-island schooners unloading their cargoes of plantains to the cheerfully bustling crowds of hucksters. The forty-foot yacht moored alongside one of the picturesque shrimp boats struck the only note of incongruity, its sparkling white paintwork and luxury fittings too new to have acquired any real tang of the sea. A man leaned idly against the door of the wheelhouse. Tessa felt his eyes following her as she passed, and had to admit that the suit did something for her that jeans and a shirt had not. She was tempted to turn round when she reached the corner where she turned off to make her way up to Broad Street, but she resisted. Just suppose he was still looking. How would she feel then?

The few items on her list did not take long to obtain, but for once Tessa found herself in no hurry to get back. She dawdled outside Stecher's to gaze at the displays of jewellery and crystal with admiring but uncovetous eyes, wandered through Da Costa's various departments and accepted a spray of expensive French perfume from the tester with no intention of buying. She was fingering a length of Thai silk and trying to visualize it as a dress when she became aware of the man standing a few yards away watching her. When she looked up he smiled, hitching the reefer jacket he was carrying more comfortably across his shoulder. In the white slacks and shirt, with a cap set at a jaunty angle on his blond head, he looked more like a fugitive from a film set than a real flesh and blood sailor, but there was no denying his rakish good looks, or the sudden little flutter inside Tessa's chest as her eyes met the knowledgeable slaty-blue ones.

Without even thinking about it she began to walk quickly away, resisting the impulse to break into a run when she found him following her. Outside again she made a dash across the road, heard the screech of brakes, and the next moment was snatched to safety by someone whose grip around her waist was tight enough to hurt as she was carried to the far pavement.

'Do you Wrights make a habit of this?' asked an all too familiar voice in her ear as she was set back fairly and squarely on her feet. 'It's about time you learned to look before you leap.'

Tessa looked up into Bryn's exasperated face and tried to regain control over her quivering nerves. Talk about out of the frying-pan into the fire! She might have done better to stay and take her chances with the yachting type. A swift glance across the road revealed no sign of the latter. No doubt he had given up the chase long before she even emerged from the store.

'Now what?' asked Bryn, following her eyes. 'Somebody after you, or something?'

'No,' she denied a little too quickly, saw his eyes narrow a fraction and added with haste, 'I thought I'd dropped something, that's all. You didn't have to be so rough!'

The lift of the mobile left eyebrow was sarcastic. 'I didn't have time to consider the niceties, unfortunately. Another second or two and you'd have been under that truck. Where were you going in such an all-fired hurry?'

'To the Wharf to get the car,' she said without pausing for reflection.

'In this direction? You'd find it a bit of a long way round.' He studied the cream suit for a moment, came back to her face with an expression in his eyes she couldn't fathom. 'If you've that much time to spare how about having a drink with me? There used to be a little bistro just round the corner from here, if memory serves me right. I could use a cold beer.'

With lemonade for her, no doubt, Tessa reflected, but found herself nodding her agreement even as the thought passed across her mind. She fell into step beside him, clasping her parcels more securely under her arm and trying not to break into a trot to keep up with his longer stride. Out of the corner of her eye she could see the way his knitted cotton shirt fitted tightly across his chest, its orange-red hue no more out of place here in the sunshine than the flamboyant itself. Bryn was the kind of man who attracted attention without even trying, she acknowledged, intercepting some of the female glances he was drawing. He didn't appear to be taking any particular notice, but he was probably perfectly well aware of the impression he created. She imagined it would amuse him. For some reason that thought brought a faint depression.

The bistro Bryn had referred to was still in operation, though under new management since his last visit. He ordered fruit punch for Tessa and beer for himself, emphasizing the 'cold' in a way which brought a nod and a grin from the young waiter. The drinks arrived in glasses taken straight from the refrigerator and still frosted with ice round the rim. Bryn raised his to his lips, took a long appreciative swallow and set it down again with a grunt of satisfaction.

'I'd forgotten just how good that was,' he observed across the width of the small wooden table. 'It was worth coming back just for this moment alone.'

Tessa ran a finger round the rim of her glass and licked the ice off it, caught his ironical glance and vexedly regretted the habit. Trust her to do something like that with Bryn watching! She picked up her drink, avoiding his eyes as she sipped at it with rather more restraint than usual. If she was to convince him that she was no longer the kid he'd known five years ago then she had to start thinking before she said or did anything. And it was somehow important that he should be convinced.

'I like the perfume,' he commented on a light note. He reached over and took her wrist in his hand, bringing it across the table and up to his face. 'French, isn't it?' He sniffed again, his lips seeming almost to brush the soft inner skin. 'Guerlain, I think. That's a very expensive brand.'

'I was just trying it out.' Tessa almost snatched the hand back, her skin tingling to his touch, her heart suddenly beating double time. 'Obviously I can't afford to buy it myself.'

'Obviously.' His regard was taunting. 'I thought perhaps someone had given it to you. It's the kind of things girls do get given – by boy-friends, maybe?'

The only person she knew likely to give that sort of present to a girl was Val Wyman, Tessa reflected dryly. And *he* would only do it if the girl in question happened to be special to him, she was pretty certain of that. On her last birthday Blake had given her the new snorkel and mask she had been wanting, and Rob a pair of flippers. She had been thrilled to bits with them at the time, yet now she found herself suddenly wishing they had found something a little more feminine for once. She hadn't known Val then, of course – or at least, only as a name. Perhaps on her next birthday in three weeks' time he might just fulfil that wish. Being twenty was very much different from just adding another year in the teens. It was supposed to be a milestone, wasn't it?

'Perhaps when I start work I'll be able to buy myself all sorts of things like this,' she said with deliberation, and was rewarded by the swift change of expression in the lean features opposite.

'What kind of work?' he queried.

'Oh ...' she gave a little shrug ... 'I'm thinking of taking a job with Wyman's.'

His regard was quizzical. 'Because of what I told you last night?'

Tessa had the grace to colour a little. 'Partly,' she admitted. 'If I'd known things were so tight I'd have done something about it before now, but ...'

'But under the circumstances you're just going to do your best to rectify the omission,' Bryn's tone was dry. He looked at her for a long moment, then gave a sigh and shook his head. 'Tessa, you're grasping at straws. Even if you do get a job ...' he held up a resigned hand as she opened her mouth to protest ... 'all right, *when* you get a job, it isn't going to bring in enough to make up for the decrease in the family income *and* buy you luxuries like that perfume. You must realize that much.'

'All right, so it won't.' Tessa refused to be deflated. 'I've managed up till now without things like this, so I'll hardly feel deprived.'

'Anything to keep Greenways, eh?' His gaze sharpened. 'Or would it be nearer the mark to say anything to keep me from getting it?'

It was too near the mark for comfort, but Tessa had no intention of admitting it. 'I'm not giving it up,' she said. 'Not without at least trying to keep it going.' She made herself look him straight in the eye. 'Last night you accused me of being too selfishly concerned with having a good time. You should be feeling gratified that the message went home.'

'Fine – except that I don't happen to think this is the answer.' He sounded irritated. 'I'm surprised your mother even considered it – if she knows yet.'

'She knows. She thinks it's a good idea, providing I'm happy doing it. And I'm sure I shall be.' Her eyes were sparkling. 'Val will be only too glad to find me something when he knows the position.'

Some new expression invaded his gaze. 'You know the Wymans well?'

'Oh, Val's an old friend,' with an airy gesture intended to convey far more than that. 'I'll put it to him on Saturday when I see him.'

'At the party?'

'Yes.' She looked at him sharply. 'Are you going?'

His smile was mocking. 'I've been invited. This morning. News travels fast in this place.' He glanced at his watch, drained his beer and put the glass down again on the table. 'I've got an appointment in twenty minutes. That just gives me time to walk you back to the car.'

'I don't need an escort,' she responded, pushing away her own half empty glass and getting up all in the same movement. 'You seem to forget I've lived here most of

50

my life.'

'Maybe. But as you're not prepared to tell me what you were diving across the road like that for, an escort is what you're getting. If you want to argue about it you can do it back at the car.' He put a couple of bills down on the table, told the boy to keep the change and led the way out into the street again with the air of one who was going to have his own way or know the reason why.

This time they cut down Higginson Lane to the car park, thereby avoiding that part of the Wharf where the yacht was moored, much to Tessa's relief. Yet she had to confess to a secret gratification that a man like the blond-haired stranger had found her attractive enough to follow at all. Clothes certainly made a difference.

'I'm quite sure I'll be safe enough from here,' she said with unconcealed sarcasm when she was in the Morris. 'Thanks for the drink.'

'My pleasure.' Bryn stepped back from the window with a jeering smile as she put the vehicle into gear. 'Drive carefully, honeychild. If the family income is going to depend on you you'd better start having a regard for life and limb!'

Tessa left him standing there, shooting out of the park and turning left into Hinks Street with all the acceleration she could muster, narrowly avoiding another vehicle coming through from the other intersection. The driver applied brakes and horn with just about equal pressure, causing every head to turn right down the street. In her mirror Tessa saw Bryn appear at the corner to stand looking after her and shaking his head. She could imagine what he was thinking and didn't care a jot. Drive carefully indeed!

CHAPTER THREE

TESSA avoided Bay Marris during the following few days, aware of a sharp reluctance to put herself in the way of Bryn's sarcastic comment again. Yet she was also aware of a certain restlessness, a feeling that the life which up until now had completely satisfied her was somehow lacking in motivation. She was getting older, of course, and nothing remained static, but deep down she knew that somewhere a door had closed on the day Bryn Marshall had returned to Barbados, and a new one was yet to open. She only hoped that wherever it led her the way would be free of clashes with that particular individual.

She spent most of Saturday water-skiing and scuba diving with Blake and Rob Summers and one or two others of their crowd. They were both sports she could not have afforded to indulge in herself, but she had known the Summers far too long to have any embarrassment over borrowing their equipment. She had been skiing only since the previous month, and by no means considered herself an expert, but where skin-diving was concerned she could hold her own with any of the boys in the group.

Today, because of the presence of two learners, they stuck to the fringe reef, playing around between the huge heads of brain coral until the daisy-like tube worms were dizzy with the effort of keeping out of sight. Fish were everywhere, colourful and exotic; jaunty sergeant-majors with their black and yellow stripe; the odd-looking trumpet fish; angel fish of so many shades and hues they defied description, and all so tame they would eat out of the hand.

It was a tired but satisfied party which eventually made their way back to the shore to sprawl in contented heaps over the sand in the late afternoon sunlight.

'Pity you have to go to this Wyman affair tonight,' grumbled Blake mildly when he finally roused himself to start gathering the gear together. 'You'll be on your own so far as our crowd is concerned. The folk are going, of course.'

'I'll survive, I suppose,' Tessa said lightly, unwilling to reveal the part of her that was actually looking forward to the evening. Some only half understood instinct bade her add, 'Anyway, Val isn't likely to park me with the older folk.'

'Might be better if he did,' commented one of her female companions without lifting her head from its supine position. 'The one time I had a date with him I was bored almost to tears! Val was born serious. 'Tisn't his fault, I suppose, but it sure makes life miserable for others.'

The remark had a vaguely deflating effect, but not enough to completely ruin Tessa's mood of anticipation. When Blake dropped her off at the end of the lane leading up to Greenways she was keyed up enough to take the remaining distance at a run, arriving breathless and dishevelled on the veranda just as her mother came out from the living-room.

'I thought you'd begun to quieten down a little,' observed the latter, viewing the creased and stained jeans and crumpled orange shirt with not a little distaste. 'I hope you haven't been into town like that.'

'No, we came straight through from the beach.' Tessa threw the satchel which had held food for the day on to a rattan chair and stretched luxuriously. 'I suppose I'd better think about getting changed. Are you driving down, or shall I?'

'We're not taking our car,' Shirley said steadily. 'Roland is sending one up for us.' She was half turning away as she spoke. 'I was just going to start getting ready myself, only I wanted to make sure you were back first. It wouldn't have been unlike you to get here too late to go.'

Tessa had to acknowledge the truth in that. But not tonight. Tonight was special, although just why it should be so she wasn't prepared to go into just yet. The changes taking place inside her were too new and too precarious to stand any kind of analysis.

She was ready and waiting by ten minutes to the hour, a slender young figure in crisp lemon cotton with narrow shoe-string straps. She had even considered taking up her hair, but after experimenting with the springing thickness once or twice had sensibly decided to leave well alone and brushed it until it fell in shining obedience to her bare shoulders. She wore no jewellery apart from a slim silver bracelet which was her only genuine piece, but she had made one concession to the occasion in the form of a light application of blue shadow – borrowed from her mother's dressing-table – to her lids.

Shirley was already in the living-room when Tessa went out. She looked slim and amazingly young in the apricot crêpe-de-chine which had been Oliver Wright's favourite. She looked Tessa over approvingly, raised her brows faintly at the shadow, but made no comment other than 'Lovely, dear.'

The car arrived promptly at eight, whisking them in silken luxury down to the coast road, and from there to the little private bay where the Wymans had their home. The villa was built in the Spanish style with arched entrances and fretted iron window grilles, shaded by the palms which fringed the beach beyond it. The huge lounge which occupied half of one jutting wing was already thronged with people, the men resplendent in white tuxedos, the women vying to outdo one another in the matter of both dress and jewellery. Tessa saw her mother's hand go almost involuntarily to her throat to touch the single strand of pearls nestling there, as if she drew comfort from the fact that they were at least real. For herself she could not have cared less, but it hurt to realize that her mother might be feeling at a disadvantage among this crowd. Perhaps that was one of her reasons for being reluctant in the past to accept formal invitations. If so she had no need, Tessa told herself with conviction. With or without adornment, she was still just about the best-looking woman of her age in the place!

Roland Wyman came to greet them, his thin ascetic features alight with genuine warmth.

'Shirley – Tessa – I'm so glad you could both make it!' He took the older woman's hand, drawing it through his arm in a way which brought a sudden tautness in Tessa's chest. 'Come and say hallo to a few people you haven't met before. Tessa, I see Val coming over. I'm sure we can leave you young folk to take care of yourselves.'

Tessa watched the two of them move away, recognizing the difference Roland Wyman's welcome had made to her mother's attitude. She swallowed on the hard little lump in her throat, trying to consider the notion edging into her mind fairly and rationally. It was only a few days since she had said that she wouldn't mind if her mother got married again, and at the time she had really meant it. It was only now, with the possibility of Roland Wyman's intentions going beyond the realms of friendship, that she found herself viewing the prospect with some dismay. She liked Val's father well enough, but he was hardly what she had had in mind when considering the kind of man who might prove suitable. He was *too* rich, for one thing, though she supposed that could hardly be considered a disadvantage.

She caught herself up at that point. Wasn't she being a bit premature, reading so much into so little? So what if Mr. Wyman did like her mother? That didn't necessarily mean that he wanted to marry her. Did it?

Val arrived at her side, his palish brown eyes pleasantly admiring. He was a little above medium height, slenderly built and fair, with a well shaped, sensitive mouth his most distinguishing feature. Even when he smiled, as now, his face always retained a trace of seriousness. Tessa had never seen him really let go with a laugh, like Blake or Rob Summers were wont to do when something amused them. She had a feeling that Val secretly considered such exhibitions of mirth a bit vulgar. All the same, she didn't dislike him. At twenty-five he was certainly the most considerate of all the young men she was so far acquainted with.

'Thanks for coming, Tessa,' he said with flattering sincerity. 'I was afraid you might change your mind at the last minute. What would you like to drink?'

A woman nearby was holding a glass of the frothy pale green concoction which was the result of mixing crême-de-menthe and milk. On impulse Tessa said, 'I'll have a grasshopper, please. I've never tried one before.'

Val took her across to the bar and personally supervised the mixing himself, handing the glass to her and waiting for her approval in a way which gave her no heart to admit that she didn't care for the taste. She smiled instead, said, 'It's quite delicious,' in a voice which sounded, to her ears at least, quite false, and turned casually about to find herself looking straight at Bryn. He was standing with a group a few feet away, arm lightly imprisoned in the grasp of a woman who had her back to Tessa. It was a particularly lovely back, smooth and evenly tanned, shown off to the greatest advantage by the low sweep of her emerald gown. Her glossy dark hair was piled high in an elaborate style which Tessa privately considered a bit overdone in this setting. She saw a classic profile turn towards Bryn with a smile and a murmured comment, saw his mouth widen in easy response and felt a hard knot slowly forming inside her.

'Beautiful, isn't she?' Val spoke with an almost clinical detachment. 'Thea Ralston. She's staying with the de Sousas. Bryn Marshall travelled over on the same plane the other day from New York. From the way she's hanging on to him I'd say he's made quite an impression in a short time.'

'Yes.' Tessa infused a brightness into her voice. 'Do you think we could go outside for a bit, Val? There's something I'd like to talk to you about.'

If he was surprised by the request he kept it to himself. 'Of course.'

Tessa took the opportunity to deposit her glass on a table in passing as they moved across the crowded room. Sliding glass doors gave on to a covered veranda, which in turn opened out on to the flat terrace with an oval swimming pool in its centre. Beyond that lay the beach itself, shaded by palms through which the sea gleamed silver in the moonlight against the shadowed white sand. The cicadas were loud and fluid, reducing the incessant chattering of voice from within to a mere murmur. So far they were the only ones out here, but how long the solitude would last was anyone's guess.

Tessa sat down on the low wall separating terrace from beach, and gazed through the trees towards the long low line of the jetty, with the white shape of the Wymans' launch riding gently at its far end. Now that the moment had come she found herself uncertain of just how to broach the subject. The best way seemed to be to take the bull directly by the horns.

'Val,' she said, 'I need a job. Can you help?'

There was rather a lengthy silence before he answered, and when he did his voice sounded rather odd. 'Surely there's no necessity to go that far, Tessa?'

'I'm afraid there is. Or there very soon will be.' She looked up at him with a smile and a shrug. 'The crunch had to come some time. It's my own fault that I didn't realize it earlier. Anyway, it's time I started doing something with my life – something worthwhile, that is. I've had it too easy for too long. The trouble is, I'm not sure what kind of thing I can do. Do you have any ideas?' She flushed a little at the obvious hesitation in his face. 'Whatever it was I'd pull my weight, Val, you could be sure of that. I'm pretty quick at picking things up, if that's what's worrying you.'

He shook his head. 'Finding you a job wouldn't be difficult. We need someone in the personnel office, as it happens, and you'd probably be ideal. It's just that . . .' he paused again, bit his lip . . . 'I shouldn't really tell you this, but under the circumstances I can't see any other way. You don't have to worry about taking a job, Tessa. Neither Dad nor I realized things were quite so bad for you, but after this he'll probably decide not to wait any longer.'

The tightness was back in Tessa's chest. 'What are you trying to say?' she asked, low-toned.

'Simply that he plans to ask your mother to marry him. He told me about it yesterday. The only reason he's taking his time is because he thinks you might need bringing round to the idea. I told him I was sure he was wrong, but he wouldn't listen.' Val stopped, and viewed her expression with a faint change of his own. 'You wouldn't object, would you, Tessa?'

'Not if it was what Mom wanted too.' Her voice seemed to be coming from a long distance away. 'You both seem very certain that she isn't going to say no.'

Val looked somewhat taken aback for a moment. 'It never occurred to me that she might,' he said at last. 'I imagined Dad must be reasonably sure of her feelings to let me in on it in the first place. Besides . . .' He broke off with a slight shrug.

Tessa knew what he had been going to say. Who in their right senses would refuse an offer of marriage from one of the richest and most eligible men on the island? She supposed he had a point, though she doubted that any amount of financial worry would have made her mother see it that way had she not cared anything for Roland Wyman. But she did care; there was no doubt left in Tessa's mind on that score. And she wanted her to be happy.

Val was watching her a little doubtfully now. 'How do *you* feel about it?' he asked at last. 'Truthfully.'

'I don't know yet,' she admitted. 'It – It's all happening so fast.'

'They've known one another several months.'

'That's not exactly what I meant.' Her smile was strained. 'I'm not all that sure what I did mean. Perhaps I do need a little time to get used to the idea.'

'Well, that's understandable.' Val hesitated. 'You won't say anything, will you? The only reason I told you was to set your mind at rest about the future.'

The future? Yes, there was that to be considered. And in a totally new light. Tessa said slowly, 'What plans does your father have, Val? I mean, where does he intend to live?'

She knew the answer before it came. 'Why, here, of course. You'll all be moving down here.' His voice lightened. 'I'm looking forward to that.'

She knew the answer to the next question too, but she had to ask. 'And what about Greenways?'

'Your house?' He sounded surprised. 'I was under the impression that Bryn Marshall was interested in extending his land in that direction. Hasn't he said anything yet?'

News certainly did travel fast round these parts, thought Tessa achingly. She made a small jerky movement up from the wall. 'We don't want to sell to him.'

'You mean you didn't. Obviously the position is different now.'

'No!' The cry was wrong from her. She saw the astonishment in his eyes and made an attempt to get a hold of herself. 'I'm sorry. I know I'm probably not being very rational about this, but it's all come as a bit of a shock. I knew Mom might get married again some day, only I somehow never thought about living anywhere else but at Greenways.'

'Well, no, it's your home, and you're naturally fond of it.' Val's tone was reasonable. 'But you have to think about it now, Tessa. Obviously you can't expect my father to move in there.'

Tessa wished he would stop using that word. To her nothing was obvious. She felt totally confused. 'I suppose,' she said with pride, 'it wouldn't be good enough.'

'To be quite truthful, no, it wouldn't. It's a nice little place, but ...' He left the sentence there, taking her cold hand in both of his and holding it between them in a gesture that was almost an appeal. 'Tessa, try to see things sensibly. Selling Greenways is the only thing to do, and Bryn is a ready-made buyer. Living down here on the coast you'll have a great time – I'd see to that. We get along so well, and there's such a lot you miss being stuck way up there all the time.'

There was even more she would miss being stuck

down here all the time, reflected Tessa with a feeling of being rushed along too fast to think properly. What about her present friends? Where would they fit into such a life? Living in the Wyman home she would hardly be able to come and go with quite the same freedom she had been used to.

She withdrew her hand from Val's on a surge of emotion that was almost panic. 'We shouldn't even discuss this at all until everything is settled. Let's just forget I mentioned a job and leave it all for another time.'

'You're probably right.' As always he was ready to be agreeable. 'It's up to father to make the whole thing official.'

If her mother agreed, thought Tessa on a quick surge of hope just as swiftly stilled by the recollection of her face on seeing Roland earlier. She mustn't begrudge her this chance of renewed happiness. Roland Wyman could give her so much. It would be she herself who would be like a fish out of water in a place like this. If only there were some way she could stay on at Greenways, some way of persuading her mother to let her stay there alone if necessary. It was a forlorn hope, but it was the only one she had.

'Seems like we're not the only ones with a yen to look at the moon,' drawled a voice behind them. 'This is some place you have here, Val.'

'Thank you,' he returned pleasantly. 'Nice of you to say so.'

The American woman was younger than Tessa had first imagined: certainly no more than the late twenties, and just as beautiful from a full face view as her profile had suggested. Tessa's glance went briefly and involuntarily from the lovely violet eyes to the cool grey ones of the man at her side, dropping before the thoughtful appraisal he was resting on her face. Bryn had guessed something was wrong; he was altogether too good at guessing.

She said, 'We were just going back in.'

'Not on our account, I hope.' Without appearing to move Bryn was suddenly between her and the villa. He went on easily, 'Thea, I'd like you to meet another of my neighbours, Teresa Wright – Thea Ralston.'

'Hi there. I already met your mother inside.' Her smile had charm, though the gaze which flicked over Tessa's bare shoulders and slender curves held some speculation. 'I can see the resemblance. Bryn tells me you use the pool at Bay Marris quite a lot. Perhaps I'll see you there.'

This time Tessa had the sense not to look at Bryn. 'Perhaps. Are you here for long?'

'A month. Maybe more. Depends how things go.' Thea sent a slanting glance Bryn's way. 'You told me I'd not regret paying the island a visit, and I must say you've not been wrong up to now.'

'There's a lot of it still to see,' he returned on a light note. 'These two know it a whole lot better than I do. We might consider getting up a foursome for a day.'

Val looked as if he thought that might be a good idea too. 'We'd have to make it a week-end,' he said. 'I'm rather tied up other times. But I'm sure Tessa and I would be only too glad to take you round the island.'

'Wonderful!' Perhaps it was only to Tessa's ears that the exclamation sounded a little forced. There was certainly nothing of that nature revealed in Thea's expression as she slipped an arm through Bryn's in a gesture both casual and subtly intimate. 'I'd love a walk along the beach. Would you mind?'

He inclined his head, mouth pulling into the same smile he had bent on her earlier. 'I'll make allowances.'

'Big of you.' Thea lifted a hand to the two still standing by the wall as they turned towards the far end of the terrace where a step dropped down to the sand. 'Be seeing you.'

'She's not quite what you'd expect, is she?' commented Val when the other couple were out of earshot. 'I mean, personally I always somehow expect women who look like she does to be a bit – well, you know what I mean. Thea is so natural.'

Tessa wasn't sure she agreed with that latter statement, but neither was she prepared to enter into any discussion over it. She watched Bryn reach up to hold back an overhanging frond of the palm under which they were passing, and turned abruptly away. 'Shall we go back indoors?'

The first person she saw on re-entering the room was the stranger from the yacht who had followed her into Da Costa's the other day. He was wearing a tuxedo with a startlingly bright purple dress shirt, and managed to look more theatrical than ever as he leaned up against the nearest wall. He also looked decidedly bored until he saw Tessa coming in from the terrace with Val at her back.

'Well, hallo!' he said, straightening his position. 'I was beginning to think you must have been a visitor to the island like myself.'

'You two know one another already?' Val sounded disconcerted. 'I thought you said this was your first visit to Barbados, Eric?'

'So it is. Your young friend and I bumped into one another in Bridgetown my first morning.' The explanation was quick and slick. He added pointedly, 'We never got round to exchanging names.'

'Eric Varley – Teresa Wright,' the younger man obliged. 'Eric is a friend of some friends of ours in Caracas,' he explained to Tessa. To Eric himself he tagged on politely, 'The Azores from here, I think you said.'

'Unless I change my mind.' The slaty-blue eyes slid over Tessa in frank approval. 'This place has a lot to offer.'

One of the white-coated house-servants approached Val discreetly to say he was wanted on the telephone. With some obvious reluctance he went to take the call, saying he wouldn't be long. Left alone with the handsome newcomer, Tessa racked her brains to think of some intelligent remark, and could only come up with, 'Is this purely a pleasure trip you're making, Mr. Varley?'

'Mostly. Though I always keep a weather eye open for any worthwhile business proposition. I'm in exports,' he tagged on, forestalling her next question. 'And the name is Eric.'

Her answering smile was still a little reserved. There was something about this man which made her faintly uneasy, although his manner was pleasant enough. He was in his early thirties, she judged, and well seasoned, no doubt. Men of his age and apparent income group always were. She wished she could be at ease with him instead of standing here all tongue-tied like this.

'Where did you dash off to last Monday?' he asked suddenly and disconcertingly. 'When I got outside that store you'd vanished. I didn't intend to frighten you into running off. I was simply enjoying watching you.'

'You followed me from the Wharf,' she accused, and could have bitten out her tongue as she saw his smile widen.

'So you did notice me before? I rather thought you might have when you stuck your nose in the air and stalked round the corner. Sure, I followed you. You were the prettiest sight I'd seen since tying up. I certainly meant you no harm, though.' His eyes gleamed with an appealing humour. 'Now that we've been formally introduced you won't take off again, will you?'

Tessa had to laugh, and in doing so felt herself relax. 'I promise,' she said. 'How long do you think you *will* be staying in Barbados?'

There was something evasive in his light reply. 'I never work to any hard and fast arrangements. It depends what turns up. Come and sit down and tell me about yourself. I gather you know the Wymans pretty well?'

Somehow Tessa found herself seated alongside Eric on a deeply buttoned leather couch set within an alcove and responding to his questions with increasing confidence. Out of the corner of her eye she saw Val return and hover for a moment before someone else claimed his attention. She sensed that he didn't much care for their guest, and certainly did not approve of their tête-à-tête on the sofa. Well, that was too bad. She wasn't living here yet.

The memory of that earlier conversation brought a swift dampening of her spirits. Watching her face, Eric said softly, 'There seems to be something troubling you. Is it a private matter, or could I help?'

Tessa shook her head, regretting her momentary lapse into thoughts she preferred to forget for tonight. She was facing the terrace doors, but it was sheer coincidence that she happened to let her eyes stray towards them just at that moment. Bryn and Thea were just coming back in from the fragrant darkness, the latter wearing a particularly luminous smile on her red lips. Bryn looked as he always did, arrogantly sure of himself. As the grey eyes flicked in her direction, some instinct caused Tessa to bestow a warm glance on her companion. 'Thanks anyway, Eric.'

'Any time,' he said, 'if you look at me like that.'

Without actually turning her head, Tessa saw Bryn murmur something to his companion and then start towards them. There was a look on his face which she didn't care for very much, a certain compression about his lips which triggered her nerves. Conscious as she was of his approach, she still jumped when he spoke.

'First dance, I think we said, Tessa. They've switched the music through to the terrace.' His glance moved to the man at her side, his eyes hard as agates. 'Sorry, Varley.'

The other was eyeing him with a peculiar expression. 'Have we met before?' he asked. 'I don't seem to remember—'

'You wouldn't.' The reply was clipped. Bryn put out

a hand and drew Tessa unprotestingly to her feet. 'Excuse us.'

In some bewilderment she found herself drawn across the room and out on to the terrace again. It was no longer deserted as it had been earlier. Music played softly from some hidden source and several couples gyrated over the tiles. Bryn made no attempt to steer her among the latter, making instead for the beach. Tessa felt the heels of her sandals sink a little way into the sand as she stepped on to it, and felt Bryn's hand come under her elbow steadying her.

'I thought you said something about dancing?' she queried.

'It was the easiest way of getting you out of Varley's clutches,' he responded without looking at her. 'How long have you been acquainted with *him*?'

'Only a few minutes.' She couldn't understand his tone. 'He knows some friends of the Wymans'. *Do* you know him, Bryn?'

'We've never met. Let's just say he left a lasting impression in at least one of his ports of call.' He paused in the shadow of a coconut palm growing obliquely across their path, leaning against the pale trunk to take out a cigarette case. 'Have you started smoking yet?'

Tessa shook her head without speaking, and watched him light one for himself. She waited until he had pocketed the gold lighter before saying tentatively, 'I think I'm due more of an explanation than that.'

'Do you?' He sounded indifferent. 'Well, you're not getting it. Just take my word for it that Varley isn't your type, infant.'

'It isn't up to you to decide who I should talk to,' she

retorted, nettled. 'And don't call me infant!'

'Where your judgment is concerned that's exactly what you are. Did you ask Val about a job yet?'

Tessa didn't want to talk about that subject; she didn't even want to think about it. 'I haven't had much chance yet,' she prevaricated.

'No?' His lips had twisted. 'I thought you might have taken advantage of the opportunity while you were out here with him a while ago. Or was he another experiment you were trying out?'

'What's that supposed to mean?'

'I'd have thought it pretty obvious. You're just beginning to realize your assets when it comes to turning a man's head. The trouble is you lack discrimination. Val Wyman is a different kettle of fish from Varley, but just as incapable of the kind of light-hearted flirtation you need. I doubt if you've even been kissed up to now.'

Her cheeks warmed. 'I may be backward in your eyes, but I'm not *that* innocent!'

'There's one sure way of proving that statement.' The familiar mockery tinged his voice. 'Come and show me how experienced you are – if you dare.'

Tessa's heart gave a painful leap, then steadied again. 'I thought you just told me to learn to discriminate?'

'So I did.' A smile flicked at his lips. 'Perhaps you're wise to turn me down. The way you look tonight I might just forget myself.'

He was teasing her, and she resented it bitterly. For a fleeting moment she was almost tempted to do as he suggested, except that the few times she had been kissed had not equipped her to handle that kind of gesture with any degree of confidence. She looked at him standing there in the silver light and felt a sudden hard lump come into her throat. Bryn Marshall forget himself. That was a laugh! He knew exactly what he was doing at every step. He always had.

'Why don't you go back to your girl-friend?' she said huskily.

'I might if I thought you could be trusted not to go looking for trouble again.' Bryn settled himself more comfortably against the bole of the palm, the glowing tip of the cigarette creating an arc as he lifted it to his lips. 'Call it a neighbourly concern, if you like.' There was a pause, then he added on a different note, 'I may be wrong, but I'm beginning to think you may have changed your mind about taking that job, after all. You didn't give me a straight answer just now.'

'I haven't changed my mind – about anything.' Tessa had no intention of giving anything away. There would be time enough to talk about what was going to be done with Greenways when Roland Wyman had taken steps to put the whole matter on a proper footing. 'I just don't happen to think a party is an ideal place to discuss it.'

'That's not what you said earlier this week.' His eyes had narrowed, whether against the smoke or at his thoughts she couldn't tell. 'Try another excuse.'

'It isn't an excuse. I do want a job.'

'Then it's Val himself who's doing the hesitating. Can't say I blame him. Ten to one he already knows that it isn't going to be necessary for you to contribute to the family budget.'

She drew in a sharp little breath. 'What are you talking about?'

'Something that became more than apparent tonight when you and your mother arrived. I saw Roland's face – and hers. I'd say they both had a permanent arrangement in mind.'

She said tautly, 'What if they have? It still doesn't mean that you'll get Greenways.'

'I think it probably does.' His voice was deceptively mild. 'From your lack of surprise I gather you've seen the signs for yourself before this, and if you can gather that much you shouldn't have any difficulty in seeing how a man like Roland Wyman will look on a property like Greenways. He's a business man when all's said and done.'

'It won't necessarily be his decision. Even if my mother does marry him Greenways will still be hers.'

'And you think she might agree to you living there on your own? Even if you were old enough it wouldn't work out. The only way you're going to keep Greenways if your mother marries again is to find yourself a husband who isn't too proud to move into a ready-made home. Do you know anybody suitable?'

'I might.' It took an effort to answer him without giving way to the temper boiling over inside her. 'I'd do that rather than let you take over!'

He gave a faint sigh. 'Now you're being childish again. It was meant to be a joke.' His eyes went beyond her to the lighted villa. 'Most girls your age would give anything for the chance to live in surroundings like these. Roland's the type to dote on a daughter. Have you thought about all the advantages of being one to him?'

'Nothing is settled yet.' She said on a note almost of desperation, 'Both you and Val are taking it for granted that Mom is going to say yes before she's even been asked. All right, so she might like him a lot, but that doesn't mean she'll want to marry him.'

He looked at her long and hard. 'Don't try to ruin this for her, Tessa. She deserves another chance of happiness, and I personally believe Roland is the man to provide it for her. Weighed against that what does a house matter?'

It wasn't just a house, Tessa wanted to say, it was a whole way of life. But what was the use? He wouldn't understand. Bryn was used to change, would probably never settle in one place for all time. She doubted if he would even stay long enough to see the whole of his uncle's plans implemented if he did buy Greenways. Long enough to see the work put into progress perhaps, and then he would be off on his own pursuits. He didn't care about Bay Marris as his uncle had done. So long as it was bringing in a fair return on his investment he would probably be content to leave it in the hands of a manager.

'I've no intention of trying to ruin anything for her,' she said numbly. 'Can we go back now?'

'If you want to.' He came upright, throwing the remains of his cigarette down into the sand and grinding it out beneath his heel. 'The night's still young. We could have that dance.'

'No, thanks.' She couldn't quite conceal the bitterness. 'I'd rather not be with you any longer than I have to.'

His shrug was easy. 'One of the hazards of telling you something you don't want to hear. Have it your own way.'

She turned without another word and made for the

steps again, pausing when she reached them to take off her sandals one by one and tap the sand from them. Bryn came up behind her, waiting patiently for her to finish although there was plenty of room for him to pass. Tessa could feel him standing there, close enough to reach out and touch, but she wouldn't look at him. She only wished it were time to go home. The party had lost every last bit of its appeal.

Val greeted her with a reproachful expression as they entered the house again.

'I've been looking for you,' he said. 'I thought you were with Eric. He seems to have disappeared too.'

'He won't be far away.' It was Bryn who spoke on the same hard note he had used before in reference to the other man. 'Is he going to be here long, Val?'

'In Barbados? I'm not sure. I gather he has some business to take care of, but he didn't say how long it was likely to take.' He eyed Bryn curiously. 'Any particular reason for asking?'

'Just a passing interest.' Bryn gave Tessa a light pat on the arm. 'See you later.'

Thea Ralston was on the far side of the room talking to some man Tessa didn't know. She watched Bryn thread his way purposefully through the groups between and join them, saw Thea turn and smile, and knew that for her the other man had been but a stand-in. She could feel some sympathy for him. Against Bryn he didn't stand a chance. No one did. What he wanted he went out and got, regardless of how many obstacles stood in the way. And he wanted Greenways. Right at that moment Tessa felt that nothing would ever be right for her again.

CHAPTER FOUR

It was an almost completely silent journey home in the car Roland had once more provided. Once or twice Tessa felt her mother studying her in the darkness of the rear seat, but the latter made no comment other than to inquire once if she had enjoyed the evening. Tessa made an appropriate reply and lapsed into silence again, unable to bring herself to make conversation wholly for the sake of it. Her mother was happy; she could sense that much. She wondered if Roland had already spoken to her, then decided that it was unlikely. After tonight, however, when Val had told him of their talk on the terrace, he would hardly lose any time in doing so. There was no reason for him to wait. After the way her mother had responded to his company that evening he must be doubly certain of her reply.

It was after one-thirty when they finally reached the house. Shirley dispatched the car and led the way indoors, locking up behind them with a smothered yawn.

'I'm straight for bed,' she anounced. 'If I'm still there when you get up you might give me a treat and bring me a cup of tea.' Her smile was soft and youthful, lending her features a kind of inner radiance. 'It's been rather a full week-end.'

In her own room, Tessa took off the lemon dress and hung it away, then sat down before her dressing-table mirror and wiped away all traces of the eye-shadow as if by doing so she could wipe out the girl who had gone out of here so happily earlier. Shorn of its touch of sophistication her face looked younger than ever, her skin satin smooth and faintly luminous in the soft glow of the one lamp she had bothered to light, her eyelashes glistening a little from the cold cream still clinging to them. She thought of Thea Ralston, imagining the way she might look without the aids she used to such effect, and came dismally to the conclusion that with those near perfect features of hers she could be nothing else but beautiful whatever the circumstances.

Despite the lateness of the hour she was not aware of any tiredness. If she went to bed now she would lie awake for hours staring at the ceiling while her thoughts ploughed over the same ground time and time again. What she needed was something to tire her physically so that she wouldn't be able to stay awake. There had been odd times in the past when she had felt such a need. On those occasions she had usually slipped out to Bay Marris and swum in the pool until she had achieved the desired state of sleepiness. Bryn had still been at the Wymans' when they had left, and had shown no sign of immediate departure. In any case, he would probably be taking Thea back to the de Sousas' before coming home himself, which would give her more than enough time for the swim she suddenly craved. Something in her shied away from the image of the lovely dark-haired American sitting at Bryn's side in the car as they winged their way through the star-bright night. On the face of it those two suited one another admirably, both well accustomed to the kind of life Tessa might well have to contemplate herself before long.

She got up quickly and pulled out a white bikini from a drawer, slipping into it with the ease of long custom. With a short towelling robe over her shoulders she went swiftly and quietly out to glide through the darkened living-room and open up the veranda doors.

The grass sprang beneath her bare toes as she made her way up the slope to the fence and dropped down on to the path which led through wild banana and breadfruit trees to the more cultivated part of the grounds. The night was still, and, apart from the ever-present sound of the cicadas, quiet. Once out of the trees there was enough light to see her way clearly through the lush overhanging shrubbery to the pool.

Tessa left her robe draped over the curved top rail of the iron ladder and slid into the water with a small sigh of pleasure at the feel of liquid coolness on her skin. She swam end to end of the pool three times, using a crawl designed to drain the energy from her limbs in short order, then switched to a long slow breast-stroke for another couple of lengths before finally coming to a rest on her back for a few minutes under the spangled Caribbean sky. She had no idea what time it was by now, and no particular interest in finding out. The swim had tired her limbs, but her mind was as active as ever. It was no use. This wasn't going to work either. The only way she was going to get any sleep tonight was to find some answer to the problems besetting her.

But where did she start? The only possible way to keep Greenways off the market was for the three of them to go on living there themselves, and in the light of the knowledge she had gained this evening that was going to be unlikely, to say the least. She thought about her conversation with Bryn on the beach, recalling his apparently jesting suggestion that she should find herself a husband willing to accept a ready-made home. Even if she had known someone like that whom she wanted to marry it would have been no solution because Greenways didn't belong to her personally, and she doubted very much that her mother would look favourably on such a suitor. What was needed was someone who could afford to buy it, only if she had to marry such a person to gain her end it might be more ...

The sound of a car engine impinged suddenly on her consciousness, bringing her upright in the water with a motion careless enough to almost send her under. There was a brief flash of headlights through the evergreens, then the curve of the drive had taken the car along the front of the house. The engine was cut; there came the faint sound of a door closing, then everything was as it had been before.

Either Bryn had been very quick in taking Thea home, or she had been here in the pool a lot longer than it seemed, Tessa reflected. In any case, it was time to go. It was unlikely that Bryn would take it into his head to come down here at this time of night, but just knowing that he was right there in the house made her somehow anxious to get away.

She struck out for the side of the pool, hauling herself up the steps to stand for a moment on the side looking towards the pale shape looming through the trees. It might even have been worth losing Greenways for the opportunity to live right there in Bay Marris had Waldron's plans reached fruition. It had been her second home for so many years, and she loved it almost as much as he had done. But it was no use dwelling on the 'if onlys'. Waldron was dead and everything had changed.

The blur of white moving on the rear veranda brought her heart thudding into her throat. Bryn must have gone through to the library and caught a glimpse of her from the windows; at any rate, he was descending the steps in this direction. With a haste she could not have fully explained at that precise moment, Tessa made a grab for her robe, failed to get a proper hold on it and felt it slide through her fingers into the water. Bryn was coming through the trees now, his tuxedo standing out against the dark foliage. Without pausing to consider the unreasonableness of her actions, Tessa slid silently into the cover of the neighbouring shrubbery crouching there in the hope that he would accept the evidence of his eyes when he saw the pool empty.

He passed within a couple of feet of her to stop and survey the expanse of silver-dappled water. He looked very big in the moonlight, his shoulders powerful beneath the perfect fit of his jacket. His head moved slowly from left to right as he brought his gaze in and down, then he was crouching on bent knees to reach in and fish up the towelling robe, holding it drippingly aloft for a moment before sending his glance searching across the width of the pool.

'All right, Tessa,' he said. 'Come on out. I know you're there.'

It was the note of tolerant amusement in his voice which fired Tessa into action, catapulting her out from her hiding place with all the speed and agility of her lithe young body to place a foot squarely in the small of his back and push with all her might. Taken totally by surprise as he must have been, he went in cleanly, cleaving the water with scarcely a splash and surfacing almost immediately a few feet out. Tessa stared at the dark head as it came round to face her, her limbs suddenly losing all capacity to move from the spot as the realization of what she had done swept over her. What on earth had possessed her? And with Bryn, of all people! She must have been mad!

He was moving towards the side now, making for the ladder clamped to the stonework a foot or so away from where Tessa stood. Even as he pulled himself up with one hand he was stripping off his sodden jacket with the other, allowing it to fall in a heap at his feet when he gained the pool edge.

Tessa saw his face in the pale clear light and felt life return to her limbs on a surge of panic which whipped her round and away in a blind attempt to escape the nemesis about to fall on her. She could hear Bryn coming after her, but dared not look back to see how close he was. She could remember him angry in the past, but never quite like this. She hated to think what he might do to her if he caught her – only he wasn't going to catch her. She knew every inch of these grounds and he didn't. That was her advantage. Once she reached the denser growth of trees beyond the gardens she would be able to lose him easily enough.

It was the mules she had dropped the previous week which proved her undoing. Tessa felt the hard edge turn beneath her toes and was next moment sprawling her length in the grass. Before she could even sit up Bryn was upon her, rolling her over and pinning her there beneath him. The white silk shirt clung wetly to his body, outlining the muscular strength of his arms. She looked into the blazing grey eyes and made a futile attempt to break his hold on her, twisting wildly from side to side and hammering at him with her fists.

'Let me go!' she panted. 'Bryn, let me go!'

A muscle jerked suddenly at the corner of his mouth, and the expression in his eyes changed character. His hands fastened on her wrists, hauling her to her feet and swinging her bodily into his arms as he turned in the direction of the pool again. Tessa had enough sense left to take a breath before he tossed her in, but the sting of the water as she hit the surface drove most of it from her body again. She came up gasping to see Bryn standing on the side, legs astride and hands resting lightly on hips in a stance which threatened further violence should she care to try him.

'Come on out,' he said.

He kept pace with her along the side as she moved towards the ladder, ignoring the squelching ruin of his shoes. Lacking the courage to refuse the proffered hand, she found herself hauled bodily up the iron rungs and set dripping on her feet in front of him, her eyes level with the bedraggled black bow tie now hanging loosely down his shirt front.

'If there's one thing I should have learned to expect from you it's the unexpected,' he said. 'You never heard of Queensberry rules. Anyway, I'd say we were about quits. You'd better come and get dry before you get off home. I'll lend you a robe. Your own seems to have suffered the same fate as everything else round here tonight.'

Tessa looked at him then, to have her gaze levelly returned. Not exactly friendly, but not really angry either any more. 'I'll be dry by the time I get home,' she muttered.

'Possibly, but you're still coming back with me first,' he said without change of tone. 'If your mother has woken up and missed you she'll want an explanation – although I don't suppose this is the first time you've slipped out in the middle of the night.'

He didn't wait for an answer, if an answer was called for at all, turning her about with a hand on her shoulder and urging her in the direction of the house, pausing only to pick up both his jacket and her robe in passing.

They entered the house via the library, passing through to the hall and stairs. The air had dried both of them enough to stop any drips, but Bryn's shoes left damp patches wherever he trod. He showed Tessa into the guest bathroom, indicating the thick yellow towels over the rail.

'Rub yourself down,' he said. 'I'll find you a robe.'

Tessa stripped off the limp bikini and wrapped herself in one of the huge soft towels, clutching it grimly about her as Bryn came back with a plain white bathrobe in his hands.

'You might have knocked!'

'I told you I was fetching this.' He slung the robe over the stool and went out again, this time closing the door right to behind him.

It took Tessa only a minute or two to towel herself dry, but her hair was another matter. She contented herself with a brisk rub, and left it to hang about her shoulders, refusing even a brief glance in the mirror because she could well imagine what she must look like. The robe swamped her, but its very bulk seemed to offer some measure of security, though against what exactly she wasn't entirely sure. The churning feeling was back inside her. She wanted badly to get out of Bay Marris, and yet some other small part of her wanted just as badly to stay. She only wished she could sort out what she did feel right now.

Bryn was coming out of the bedroom opposite when she emerged, fastening the buttons of a fresh cotton shirt. His hair was rough dried and looked as though he had just put his fingers through it. His eyes flickered over her without change of expression.

'Right,' he said, 'we'll get you back where you belong before Josh comes to see what's going on.' There was irony in the line of his mouth. 'I've enough to answer for in his view without adding to the list.'

With the damp ball that was her bikini clutched in her hand, Tessa accompanied him downstairs again and out by the same way they had entered the house a few minutes earlier. Bryn fell into step beside her, slowing to her own pace and helping her over the rougher patches.

'Sorry I couldn't provide you with shoes too,' he commented at one point. 'We should have picked up those you fell over.'

'It doesn't matter, I'm used to going barefoot.' Tessa added staunchly, 'I suppose I should say I'm sorry for pushing you in the pool.'

'Except that it wouldn't be true.' His eyes glinted a little as he cast a glance her way. 'One of these days those impulses of yours are going to land you in real trouble. Next time you have a beef try talking about it, will you?' He waited a moment for some reply, then gave a sigh. 'Look, Tessa, it's no use taking it out on me because things aren't working out the way you'd like them to. If your mother does decide to marry Roland then the place won't be any use to her, and if I don't buy it someone else certainly will. Wouldn't you rather see it become a part of Bay Marris than have a complete stranger living there?'

'Perhaps.' The agreement was reluctant. 'What exactly would you do with the house itself?'

'Turn it into a clubhouse for the golfers. It's in an ideal spot, and there wouldn't be a lot of alteration necessary.'

Her nose wrinkled. 'That makes it worse, not better. It wouldn't even be a home any longer.'

'Oh, for God's sake!' Impatience sprang in his voice. 'You talk about it as if it were alive! What difference does it make? One house is much the same as another, as you'll soon find out once you've tried a few. That's half the trouble with you. You've not had chance to find out what life has to offer apart from kicking your heels around here. In one way it was selfish of Oliver to bring you to Barbados at an age when your horizons should just have begun to widen. It's beautiful but limiting.'

'It has everything I want or need.' Her throat felt tight and dry. 'And leave Dad out of it. He came here for the peace to write as he wanted to write, and he succeeded. If you'd ever felt deeply over anything you might have a chance of understanding his reasons, but all you're interested in is change. Well, I don't want to change, thank you. I'm happy just the way I am!'

'You need to fall in love,' he came back hardily. 'Only knowing you you'd ten to one choose somebody entirely unsuitable and end up getting hurt.' He paused. 'Will you promise me something?'

She was cautious. 'I'd have to know what it was first.'

'Just don't give Val Wyman too much encouragement, that's all, or you're going to find yourself taken over lock, stock and barrel. He's already possessive about you, I noticed.'

'You seem to have noticed rather a lot tonight,' she said with sarcasm, aware of a sense of deflation. 'Perhaps I don't mind Val being possessive about me. If he's going to be family anyway, I might even fall in love with *him*. That would make things all nice and cosy, wouldn't it?'

'Stop it.' He sounded abrupt. 'Val isn't the man for you, and you know it. If you married him you'd simply be exchanging one kind of limitation for another. He's too wrapped up in the business to make any proper time for a wife.'

They had reached the house now. All was in darkness still. Tessa stopped at the foot of the veranda steps and looked at Bryn, unable to see his features properly here in the shadows. 'Who said anything about marriage?' she asked on a deliberately flippant note. 'I thought we were talking about love.'

His smile was faint and mocking. 'Don't try to impress me that way. You'd die of fright if anyone so much as kissed you with any degree of passion.'

Had it been daylight Tessa might have felt a somewhat different reaction to that latter statement. In darkness she was conscious only of her thudding heartbeats and a sudden recklessness which made her lean a little towards him in direct challenge. 'Don't be so sure.'

He gave a short laugh, a gleam that was not wholly amusement leaping in his eyes. Then his hands were on her waist, lifting her down and into his arms, his mouth on hers in a kiss which brought the blood pounding into her head. She went rigid in his grasp, aware of sensations she had never experienced before during the few seconds that the kiss lasted, then as suddenly as he had seized her he let her go, turning her about and urging her up the steps with a slap that stung. When she looked back he was already moving away across the grass.

There was a phone call from Roland Wyman the following morning. Shirley took it in her own room, emerging some few moments later with a brightness about her face that left Tessa in no doubt as to the nature of the call.

'Roland wants to take me out to lunch,' she said. 'And Val would like a word with you, Tessa.'

'About what?' asked her daughter cautiously.

'How would I know? If you speak to him you'll find out for yourself.'

Tessa went through and took up the receiver with some reluctance. She didn't want to speak to Val this morning. She didn't want to speak to anyone, if it came to that. She felt more than a little depressed.

Val sounded his usual steady self. 'I don't think I need tell you why Dad wants to get your mother on her own,' he said, as pleased as if he had arranged the whole thing himself. 'I thought we might take a leaf out of the same book and have lunch together somewhere ourselves. I understand Oliver is spending the week-end with a friend?' He paused. 'Do you like the Hilton?'

'I've never been,' Tessa replied with truth. She felt a stirring of interest despite herself. Anything would surely be better than sitting around on her own all day. Besides, if she and Val were going to be related it was probably time they began getting to know one another a bit better. At least he wasn't complicated, like some others she could think of. She broke off that train of thought abruptly and brought her mind back to bear on the subject in hand. 'It sounds a good idea,' she said on a determinedly bright note. 'What time?'

'I'll follow Dad when he comes up to collect your mother. About noon. I'll book a table for one o'clock, then we can think about what to do afterwards.' He sounded delighted by her agreement. 'I'll be looking forward to seeing you, Tessa.'

'Me too,' she said with as much sincerity as she could muster, and rang off with a guilty feeling that she was using Val in a not very nice way.

Shirley received the news with evident pleasure but no surprise, causing Tessa to wonder if perhaps the suggestion might have originated from her in the first place. It would round things off beautifully if she and Val could be tied up as well, she reflected with a flash of cynicism, and then immediately felt ashamed because whatever happened her mother would only wish her happiness.

It was still only just after ten, leaving two hours to be got through before the Wymans were due to arrive. For the first time in her life Tessa actually found time hanging heavily on her hands. She went out to the veranda and threw herself down into a chair, read a few lines of the novel her mother had left on the floor at its side and found the words dancing before her eyes without making the least bit of sense. Eventually she gave in, and allowed her thoughts to return to the events of the previous night, feeling the quickening of her pulses at the memory of Bryn's kiss right there on the steps. If only he hadn't made it so obvious that he had done it simply to teach her a lesson. That was what hurt the most. Yet she supposed she could hardly blame him for treating her like a schoolgirl. Kicking him into the pool hadn't exactly been adult behaviour.

Involuntarily her gaze turned towards Bay Marris, invisible though the house was behind the trees which sheltered it. He was up there now, back on the island just a week and already a source of heartache again. Hadn't she learned anything in five years? *He* hadn't changed; he never would. To Bryn she was still the kid next door who had once had such a crush on him; he probably thought she still had. Tessa wished with all her heart that she could dismiss the way she felt about him now as lightly as that.

She was ready when the Wymans arrived, outwardly cool and composed in a crisp white cotton with a cerise scarf tying back her hair. Val's unconcealed admiration warmed her to him. It was nice to be admired, nicer still to be liked as much as he obviously liked her. She determined there and then that she was going to make every effort to be equally nice to him during the coming few hours.

Roland's greeting held a subtle difference this morning, as though he were already feeling his way into the part of stepfather to a grown daughter. He looked maturely attractive in a beige linen suit, his silvered hair lending distinction to his features. When he looked at her mother, Tessa could no longer doubt the depth of his emotion. It was there in his eyes for all the world to see, and he wasn't ashamed of it.

The two cars parted when they reached the Highway, one heading east to join the St. Philip road, the other making for Bridgetown. Val drove with concentration, leaving Tessa free to sit back and enjoy the ride. It was only the second time she had been in an open sports model, and she thought it the best way of all to travel. Let them keep their air-conditioned saloons; give her the open air any day!

'Happy?' asked Val, glancing her way with a smile.

Tessa smiled back. 'Yes.' And she was, she told herself with emphasis. Who wouldn't be in a situation like this? She had everything a girl might want: rich, attractive escort; luxurious transport, and a whole afternoon stretching before her in which to enjoy them. What more could she ask for?

The Hilton was as impressive as she had always imagined, an opulent mingling of stone and glass and dark polished wood. There was even a rock garden inside the lobby, complete with a waterfall which tinkled down between dwarf palms and other miniaturized plant life to disappear beneath the floor. The restaurant was almost full, but their table was ready for them, scintillating with silver and glass. Tessa accepted the huge menu from a smiling waiter with a feeling that she might not find this kind of life so very difficult to get used to after all, providing she could work up to it gradually. There was a lot to be said for not having to count the cost.

It took an hour to work through the various courses Val helped her choose, washed down with a sparkling white wine which inspired a definite vivacity. By the time coffee arrived Tessa was looking at Val in a new light. Given half a chance he could be very entertaining in his own way, and he hadn't once mentioned business affairs. True, he was maybe a bit lacking in humour, but that could hardly be held against him. Perhaps it was even that her own sense of humour was a trifle over-developed. One couldn't go through life making fun of everything. It was odd that until now she hadn't realized just how much Blake Summers tended to do just that.

She shook her head when Val inquired if she would like a brandy to go with the coffee.

'It just isn't me,' she admitted with a laugh. 'I'd probably fall flat on my face when I came to get up, and disgrace you.'

'I could always hold you up,' he returned, taking the remark at its face value, but he didn't press her. He added with sincerity, 'I've enjoyed bringing you here, Tessa. It's been quite a while since I last took a girl out – to enjoy it, I mean. You're so unaffected. Most of the others seem concerned only with making the right kind of marriage.'

Val was no fool, Tessa reflected. He was well aware that he was regarded as one of the most eligible bachelors on the island. Idly she tried to imagine what it would be like to be married to someone like Val. Life would probably hold few surprises, but there was something solid and dependable about him even at twenty-five. A girl might certainly do a lot worse – if she was thinking about marriage at all, that was.

As if in response to her thoughts, he suddenly reached out a hand and covered one of hers. 'I hope we're going to do this again soon. I'd like to bring you down here to the cabaret one night. There are dozens of places I want to take you.' He was almost boyish in his enthusiasm. 'Say you'll come!'

Tessa would not have been human had she failed to be flattered by his eagerness, but some small inner voice cautioned her not to commit herself too easily to his plans. She smiled at him, said lightly, 'It sounds great, Val. I've enjoyed today too.'

'It isn't over yet,' he reminded her. 'Where would you like to go from here?'

'I don't mind.' The wine was still providing enough of a glow to make her expansive. 'You choose.'

'We could take the launch out, I suppose. It's been ages since I did that.' He eyed her doubtfully. 'But you haven't brought a swimsuit, so we won't be able to go in the water.'

Tessa laughed and tapped the raffia bag at her side. 'I have one in here, just in case. What my mother calls being prepared for all eventualities!'

He laughed at that, then sobered again to say softly, 'I think my father's choice of a second wife could hardly have been bettered. Perhaps you'd like to choose a room for yourself when we reach the house? After all, it won't be so long before you're moving in permanently.'

The glow faded a little. Tessa sat up straighter, her

smile losing its spontaneity. 'I think it's a bit too soon for that,' she said, 'but I'd love to go out on the boat. Do you carry scuba equipment?'

'Yes – though I'm not all that experienced a diver myself.' Val raised a hand and summoned the waiter. 'We'll get off now and make an afternoon of it.'

The Bay Street esplanade was thronged with people watching the yacht racing out in the bay, they in turn being watched over by a couple of the island's mounted policemen in their beautiful and somewhat theatrical red, white and blue uniforms. A Sunday somnolence hung over the town itself, the few people to be seen on its streets moving with the slow indolent tread of those in no hurry to get anywhere. The tall-masted schooner used as a training ship lay berthed in Deep Water Harbour where the cruise liners disgorged their eager hordes every few days, her graceful lines recalling times long prior to those of steam and motor. The sight of her standing off in full sail was one to linger in the memory long after she had disappeared from view.

It took them a good fifteen minutes' driving to reach the bay. The first thing Tessa saw on entering the gates was the low white car parked in the open space before the villa.

'Hallo,' exclaimed Val, sounding a bit put out, 'we've got visitors. Wonder who that can be?'

'It's Bryn Marshall's car,' Tessa supplied, already wishing they hadn't bothered coming back at all. It was on the tip of her tongue to suggest that they left again before anyone knew they were there, but she quickly realized that how improbable it was that Val would agree. In any case, the car would already have been heard arriving.

Esma Layne, the Wymans' comfortably padded housekeeper, met them in the outer hall looking distinctly bad-tempered.

'A body cahn have no peace and quiet roun' here,' she complained with the familiarity of long acquaintance. 'Firs' you say everybody out till evenin', an' then everybody turn up!'

'It's all right, Esma, we're going out again on the launch,' Val placated her. 'Where is Mr. Marshall?'

'He go down to the boat with she.'

That would be Thea, Tessa realized. She said quickly, 'Let's leave them to it, Val. I'm not really bothered about diving this afternoon.'

He was frowning a little. 'I think I ought to go and see what's going on first. Just give me a minute to change.'

Tessa went out on to the veranda while she waited, standing on the edge of the terrace to look across the pool and down through the line of palms to the jetty. She could see a couple of figures on deck, although they didn't appear to be moving about. If they intended taking the launch out she hoped they would get on with it before Val arrived, regardless of whose vessel it was. One person she did not want to see today was Bryn, especially in Thea's company.

But the launch was still tied up when Val joined her, wearing a pair of shorts and a cotton shirt now. The deck was empty when they emerged from the trees and made their way across the strip of white sand to mount the little wooden jetty, but the sound of their footsteps on the slats brought someone to the hatchway to peer in their direction. Tessa felt her steps slow as Bryn's lean features registered recognition.

'Hi there,' he greeted them cheerfully. 'Your father not tell you he'd offered me the use of the boat today, Val?'

'Well, no, he didn't.' Not by a flicker of an eyelid did the younger man reveal his disconcertion. 'I suppose it didn't occur to him, seeing that it must be six weeks or more since I used it last.' He added lightly, 'It wouldn't have occurred to me to use it today if I hadn't had Tessa with me.'

Thea had come up from the cabin behind Bryn, and now stood leaning nonchalantly against the hatch. She was wearing a pair of linen hipsters in emerald green with a matching halter top. Today her dark hair was swept back from her face with a green and white bandeau. 'Seems like we all had the same idea,' she drawled.

'In which case I'd suggest that we make a foursome for the afternoon,' Bryn responded imperturbably. His eyes sought Tessa's for a moment, and he lifted a mocking brow. 'Nothing much to say for yourself today? Or is it just a disinclination to share?'

'Of course not.' Val spoke for her, a little too quickly. 'It seems like a good idea.'

Tessa decided it was time she said something – anything. 'We may not want to go the same way. Perhaps it would be better if we did something else instead, Val.'

'We were only going out for a blow, and perhaps a swim,' Bryn returned before Val could answer that one. 'Where isn't all that important. If you two had somewhere special in mind we'd fall in.' He held out a hand to Tessa. 'Jump aboard.'

There was little else she could do but obey, steeling herself for the firm grip of his fingers on hers. He caught her by the elbows as she stumbled on landing, holding her there in front of him and smiling down at her. 'Better take off those sandals, unless you want to break an ankle.'

Tessa pulled away from him without speaking, and glanced back at Val. 'I'll go down and get changed.'

The cabin was surprisingly roomy for a fairly small craft. Soft banquettes edged the panelled bulkheads, with a swinging table set between them at the far end. Immediately on her right was the tiny galley, complete with a four-ring cooker, balanced on gimbals so that a meal could be prepared even while the boat was under way. Dark blue curtains were hooked back from the portholes.

Thea had followed her down, pausing on the bottom rung to reach into a pocket of the emerald shirt hanging from a nearby hook and take out cigarettes. 'Like one?' she asked on an indifferent note.

Tessa shook her head. 'I don't smoke, thanks.'

She opened her handbag and took out the scrap of bikini, hoping that the other would take the hint and go back up top. She wasn't in the least prudish in front of other members of her own sex normally, but for some reason Thea's very presence made her self-conscious. 'I'm sorry if we barged in on your afternoon,' she offered, trying to lighten the atmosphere. 'It was a spur-of-the-moment idea.'

'Can't be helped.' Thea obviously saw no reason to

make out that she didn't really mind. Neither did she apparently have any intention of leaving the cabin as yet. Instead she leaned against the bulkhead and lit the cigarette, drawing on the smoke with the air of making the best of things. 'Don't mind me,' she added. 'I'm wearing mine.'

Tessa turned her back and reached for the zip of her dress. She could hear the men's voices overhead, and then there came the throb of the engine starting up, causing the boards to vibrate beneath her feet. 'We're off,' she said unnecessarily.

'Yes.' Thea stubbed out the barely begun cigarette and unfastened the narrow belt of her pants, stepping out of them and throwing them carelessly on to the nearest couch. Her figure was magnificent, and she knew it. It was there in the way she carried herself, in the gleam of derision in her eyes as she said, 'Shall we join the menfolk?'

CHAPTER FIVE

BRYN was at the wheel, his gaze fixed forward as he brought the launch round in a wide arc to head for the open sea. He had taken off his tan shirt and wore only a pair of shorts. The hairs on his bare arms glinted golden in the sunlight slanting in through the windshield.

'Val tells me you're eager to do some diving, Tessa,' he said without turning his head. 'Where's the best place?'

'Anywhere along this stretch,' she responded. 'But I don't have to go down today. We can always come out again some time.'

'I'll come down with you,' ignoring the last. 'I'd welcome the chance to do some diving while I'm here. There are two full tanks. I checked them before you arrived.'

'You and Val go down, then,' Tessa said quickly. 'There isn't going to be enough for more than one dive.'

'I'll stay on board, in that case,' spoke up Val. 'It isn't my favourite pastime. How about you, Thea?'

The other girl shrugged, her expression unrevealing. 'I guess I'm no water baby either. Seems like we'll be left holding the boat, Val. Do you have any drink aboard? I make a zinging rum punch!'

'There should be plenty below.' He moved to the hatch. 'I'll show you.'

They were running parallel to the coast now, cruising

Love, romance, intrigue...all are captured for you by Mills & Boon's top-selling authors.
TAKE TWO EXCITING BOOKS FREE EVERY MONTH
Romance
BLACKMAIL
Jordan
Mills & Boon
Romance
A GIRL TO LOVE
Mills & Boon
Romance
AN OLD PASSION
Robyn Donald
Mills & Boon
Romance
EDGE OF TEMPTATION
Anne Mather
Mills & Boon
Romance
BITTER-SWEET WATERS
Yvonne Whittal
See inside for details.

A Sensational Offer from largest publisher

JOIN OUR READER TAKE TWO BOOKS

Every month we publish twelve brand new Romances – wonderful books by the world's biggest names in romantic fiction – letting you escape into a world of fascinating relationships, exotic locations and heart-stopping excitement. Thousands of readers worldwide already find that Mills & Boon Romances have them spellbound from the very first page to the last loving embrace.

And now, by becoming a member of the Mills & Boon Reader Service for just one year, you can receive *all twelve* books hot off the presses each month – *but you only pay for ten.*

That's right – *two books free every month for twelve months.* And as a member of the Reader Service, your monthly parcel of books will delivered direct to your door, postage and packing free. And just look at these other exclusive benefits:

- **THE NEWEST ROMANCES** – reserve the printers for you each month and delivered direct to your door by Mills Boon.
- **POSTAGE AND PACKING FREE** – ur other book clubs, we pay all the extra You only pay the same as you would the shops.
- **14 DAY FREE TRIAL PERIOD** – you c return your first parcel of books withi fortnight and owe nothing.

Two New Books FREE EVERY MONTH

WIPE AWAY THE TEARS — atricia Lake

MAKEBELIEVE MARRIAGE — Flora Kidd

BURNING OBSESSION — Carole Mortimer

Mills & Boon – the World's of Romantic Fiction.

SERVICE AND FREE EVERY MONTH!

- **FREE MONTHLY NEWSLETTER** – keeps you up-to-date with new books and book bargains.
- **SPECIAL OFFERS,** recipes, patterns and competitions. This year our lucky winners are spending a fortnight in Barbados.
- **EXCLUSIVE BARGAIN BOOK OFFERS** – available only to subscribers.
- **HELPFUL, FRIENDLY SERVICE** from the girls at Mills & Boon. You can ring us any time on 01-684 2141.

You have nothing to lose, and a whole new world of romance to gain. Just fill in and post the coupon today.

14 DAY FREE TRIAL
Should you change your mind about subscribing, simply return your first twelve books to us within 14 days and you will owe nothing. Once you decide to subscribe, you will receive two free books each month for a full twelve months.

Mills & Boon Reader Service,
PO Box 236,
Croydon,
Surrey CR9 3RU.

FREE BOOKS CERTIFICATE

To: Mills & Boon Reader Service, FREEPOST, PO Box 236, Thornton Road, Croydon, Surrey CR9 9EL.

YES! Please enrol me in the Mills & Boon Reader Service for 12 months and send me all TWELVE latest romances every month. Each month I will pay only £9.50 – the cost of just TEN books – plus TWO BOOKS FREE. Postage and packing is completely free. I understand that this special offer applies only for a full year's membership. If I decide not to subscribe I can return my first parcel of twelve books within 14 days and I will owe nothing. I am over 18 years of age.

Please write in BLOCK CAPITALS

Name _____

Address _____

_____ Post Code _____

Signature _____ 9C3P

One offer per household. Offer applies in UK only – overseas send for details. If price changes are necessary you will be notified.

SEND NO MONEY – TAKE NO RISKS. NO STAMP NEEDED

For you from Mills & Boon:

* The very latest titles delivered hot from the presses to your door each month, postage and packing free.
* FREE monthly newsletter.

A parcel of brand new romances – delivered direct to your door every month.

Simply fill in your name and address on the FREE BOOKS Certificate overleaf and post it today. You don't need a stamp. We will then send you the TWELVE latest Mills & Boon Romances – but you only pay for TEN.

That's *two books Free* – every month!

Postage will be paid by Mills & Boon Limited

Do not affix Postage Stamps if posted in Gt Britain, Channel Islands, N Ireland or the Isle of Man

BR Licence No CN 81

Mills & Boon Reader Service,
PO Box 236, Thornton Road,
CROYDON, Surrey CR9 9EL.

at a speed which gave Tessa plenty of time to view the scenery in passing. This part of the coastline held many of the island's finest hotels, so well set among the massed evergreens and coconut palms skimming the curving beaches that from this distance whole stretches appeared as virgin territory, green against silver against a backcloth of purest blue lightly traced with white cloud.

'Beautiful, isn't it?' Bryn was watching her watching it, a smile on his lips. 'Hard to believe you're looking at the most densely populated island in the whole Caribbean. I've seen a lot of lovely spots during the last few years, but there's something about this place that sticks. It's going to be a wrench leaving it.'

She said slowly, 'When will that be?'

His shrug was noncommittal. 'I can't make any definite plans until I know where I stand with regard to buying your land. Maybe that particular hurdle will have been decided by the time today's over.'

He was probably right about that. Tessa bent her head as though looking at something in the water. 'I suppose you'll be putting in a manager?'

'I suppose I shall. It will have to be somebody reliable, and experienced. Know anyone in that line who might be looking for a change of job?'

'No, but I'll make some inquiries.'

'Thanks.' His glance held a suddenly quizzical element. 'You're being unusually helpful. Any reason for the change of heart?'

'Perhaps I'm just learning to accept the inevitable,' she came back. 'You always did get what you wanted.'

'Not always.' There was an odd note in his voice. 'There have been one or two occasions when I've had to accept the inevitable too.' He changed the subject along with his tone. 'Do you remember coming out sailing with your father the day young Oliver fell overboard?'

'And you went in after him.' Her head had lifted. 'Yes, I remember. You said kids were more trouble than they were worth.'

'Did I say that?' He sounded amused. 'I must have had a bad day. Unless I'm mistaken, you weren't even supposed to be with us. We found the two of you stowed away in the back of the car when we reached the Wharf.'

Tessa needed no nudge to bring back the details. They were etched in her memory as if it were only weeks rather than years ago. Her father had been furious, more because of the way her mother would be worrying over their disappearance than the actual prank itself. It had been Bryn who had calmed him down by suggesting that they made a quick phone call to set her mind at rest, then accept the fact that they were going to have to take the two of them along. Only nothing had gone right, and Oliver falling in the sea had been the last straw. One valuable lesson Tessa had learned from that experience was that a man deprived of his sport was apt to lose all sense of humour.

'You and Dad got on rather well,' she said after a moment. 'He had visions of the two of you walking away with all the big races that year, if you'd stayed.'

'Yes, well, that's life. It didn't work out that way.' There was a pause before he added with a curious inflection, 'Coming back isn't always a good idea either. Things are never quite as you expect them to be. Maybe I'd have done better to let someone handle the whole thing for me from here and stayed in the States myself.'

Better for her too, thought Tessa wryly. Then she could have gone on thinking of him as a man to be scorned. Talking with Bryn like this was somehow even more painful than fighting with him; especially with Thea only feet away in the cabin. She wondered if he was going to marry the American girl; there seemed to be some definite rapport between the two of them. Thea wasn't a person she could ever really like herself, but that was mostly because of the immense gulf between them. Thea was independent, worldly, confident – all the things Tessa wasn't. She was the kind of wife a man like Bryn needed. Someone capable of fitting in with his life-style.

'About here would be a good place,' she said, pushing herself abruptly away from the guardrail. 'We're right over the barrier reef. I'll get the gear ready.'

The others were coming up, Val carrying a tray with three glasses on it. Thea followed him, her own glass in her hand. She paused in the hatchway as Bryn cut the engine, watching him walk back to secure the anchor with a resigned expression.

'Guess we're going to have to drink these ourselves, Val,' she drawled. 'The kiddies are going out to play.'

Bryn grinned at her. 'Another crack like that and you might just be joining us. We'll be on our way again inside an hour.'

Tessa already had the cylinders and masks out, and

was sorting the fins into their proper pairs. She stood up as Bryn came to pick up the nearest cylinder, securing the webbing straps about her waist when he hoisted it on to her back. Fitting the rubber mouthpiece between her teeth, she adjusted the valve release until she was satisfied with the air flow, then turned it off again and took it out of her mouth. Bryn was almost ready himself by now. Tessa walked over to where the iron rungs of the ladder disappeared over the side of the boat, her fins slapping awkwardly against the planks. She spat in her mask to prevent it steaming over, leaned over the side to wash it in the water, then slipped the mouthpiece between her teeth again and fitted the mask over her face, adjusting the side clips to a comfortable tension.

Bryn was there to give her a hand up on to the gunwale. A brief pause to accustom herself to the rhythm of breathing through the tube, and then she jumped, sinking down through the sparkling green depths with the familiar sense of unrivalled delight.

At this point the reef top lay some forty feet below the surface. Tessa had reached it before Bryn caught up with her. He came alongside, touching her arm to attract her attention and pointing to the landward side of the reef in clear indication that she follow him. Cheek, thought Tessa in some indignation. She knew these waters far better than he did. She shook her head, and without waiting to see his reaction angled down the coral cliff through the middle of a school of dazzling blue chubs which parted either side of her in perfect formation. She had always loved the silky silence of the deep water, the brilliant hues of the sponges covering the coral, the gentle swaying of sea-fans and tree-like gorgonians in the current. Out here the fish were bigger than those of the inner channel, but certainly no less colourful, darting about her with curiosity but little real fear, some matching their movements to hers for whole seconds to study her with glassy eyes, others coming close enough to nuzzle an outstretched finger before darting away again in a flash of silver.

Bryn came up again, tanned body cleaving the water with powerful grace. Tessa pulled a face at him through the glass of her mask, and saw him shake a fist in mock threat. They explored the rifts and grottoes between the coral heads together, equally at home in the element. Once a turtle paddled by, its huge flippers pressing it through the water at a surprising speed. Bryn seized it by the edge of its shell and rode it for several yards, finally falling off grinning behind his mask as the turtle continued on its way unperturbed by the interruption.

Tessa felt she could have stayed down all day, but all too soon Bryn was tapping his watch face and holding up both hands with fingers extended to indicate eight minutes of air left in the tanks.

Hair streaming out from her head in a pale cloud, she turned to obey the unspoken command, launching herself forward and upward in a rhythmic leg crawl, hands along her flanks. The underside of the boat came into view like some basking sea monster sixty feet above their heads, dimming the light with its bulk. Tessa slowed to take a last look round the translucent world, allowing Bryn to pass her. It was only then that she spotted the huge tiger conch shell lying on a shelf of coral some dozen yards below her. It looked a real beauty from here, and it was so temptingly close. It would only take her seconds to go and get it.

She was half-way to the spot before she was fully conscious of making the decision, reaching out to lift the shell from its resting place and hold it towards the light to check for cracks. But there weren't any, it was perfect; a real collector's item! She could imagine how it would look as the centrepiece of her own collection at home.

Carrying it carefully in both hands, she kicked herself upwards again, and felt a sharp pain run up the back of her leg as her foot went between two jagged lips of coral. When she tried to pull it free she found herself held as fast as if she had been caught in a vice, with every movement wedging her even further into the crevice. Fear swept over her as she dropped the shell and bent to put both hands to her ankle, trying to lever the foot free from its prison. Time was at a premium by now. If she didn't get out of this before the air in her tank was exhausted ... She didn't dare dwell on that awful possibility, looking round wildly for Bryn. Why didn't he come and help her? Surely he hadn't left her down here alone? It was with a surge of relief that she saw him appear over the curve of the reef like some big brown fish. He would get her out.

But not even his lean fingers could prise her free of the crack. Face tense behind the mask, he came upright and gestured towards the boat, indicating that he was going to fetch something to use as a lever. Tessa nodded her comprehension, clutching at her control as she watched him speed upwards. Then he was gone and she was alone, fighting the kind of fear she had never experienced before. There was no spare air bottle on board that she knew. All she could rely on was what small amount remained in the cylinder strapped to her back. She resisted the urge to try extracting her foot again. It was quite useless, and the more she struggled the quicker she would use up her precious air. All she could do was wait, amidst the beauty that had suddenly become a trap, listening to the sound of her own breathing like thunder in her ears.

Thin black threads like strands of cotton were beginning to appear in the water down by her foot. Tessa knew it was blood when the fish began taking an interest. Her heart came sickeningly into her throat again, and she glanced nervously round her at the teeming life, eyes probing the far reaches. If there were any barracuda in the vicinity it wouldn't take long for them to get a scent, and even the smaller variety to be found in the area could be dangerous enough under certain conditions. It was impossible to tell how badly she was cut. The rubber strap holding on her fin was in the way. There was no pain at all, only a numbness spreading slowly up her leg. Tessa tried not to think about that either. Getting out was the most important thing.

It seemed hours but could only have been a couple of minutes before Bryn appeared. Her lift of relief on seeing him was abruptly cut short by the sight of his bare shoulders. He had left his cylinder behind, which meant that it was empty already. She tried to calculate the difference in usage between the two of them, but her brain had seized up. At the most it could only be a minute or two, and she doubted that Bryn could hold his breath for much more than half that length of time anyway.

She found she was holding her own breath as he forced the crowbar into the crevice and levered outwards, felt his hand close about her ankle in a grip that penetrated the numbness, and was suddenly rising free of the coral towards the blessed light of the sun. Bryn's arm came about her waist at the very instant that her air gave out, drawing her swiftly up to break surface at his side.

Thea and Val were two anxious faces over the side of the launch, arms reaching out to pull her up the rungs of the ladder. Bryn was close behind, taking the weight of the aqualung from her shoulders as she slipped out of the straps. He had taken off her fins in the water, and now he pressed her to a seat, to kneel down in front of her and lift her foot in his hand. The cut ran just below her ankle bone, a two-inch slash which would have been a whole lot worse but for the protection afforded by her fin. He pressed the edges to make sure that it was clean, then dried round it with a piece of clean lint taken from the first-aid box before putting on a dressing. Only then did he lift his head to look her in the eyes, his own blazing with an anger she knew was wholly deserved.

'I ought to wallop some sense into you!' he said forcefully. 'You know the rules. What the devil possessed you to turn back with only three minutes of air in your tank?'

'I saw a shell I wanted. There seemed plenty of time.' Tessa spoke in a low voice, aware that nothing she could say would excuse her action. An involuntary shudder ran through her at the thought of what might have happened down there – not only to her but to Bryn as well. He had risked his life to save hers, diving to that depth without a tank. If he hadn't been so fit he would never have made it. 'I'm sorry,' she got out. 'I shan't do that again in a hurry.'

'You'd better not do it at all – ever.' He still looked angry enough to shake her. 'If you can't use plain common sense you've no business going down at any time!'

'She already said she was sorry,' Val put in sharply. 'You don't have to go on at her!'

'Yes, I do.' Bryn didn't bother to turn his head. 'This is too important to just let slide.' He straightened, running a hand through his hair, his expression unrelenting as he looked at Tessa's pale face. 'You'd better go and get changed. Perhaps you'd go with her, Thea?'

'I don't need any help.' Tessa spoke gruffly, unable to bear the thought of being alone in the close confines of the cabin with Thea after what had happened. It had been bad enough facing his tongue-lashing with her looking on. Not that she could blame him. She had been a complete idiot.

She blinked hard on the ache behind her eyes, and pushed herself to her feet, somehow finding a smile for Val as he put out a hand to assist her. 'I'm really quite all right, honestly.'

'You're as white as a sheet.' He darted a furious glance at Bryn. 'Don't you realize what shock can do?'

'Sure,' came the laconic response. 'Just be thankful she's alive to feel it.' He took Tessa's wrist between finger and thumb, feeling for the pulse. 'A mite fast, perhaps, but strong enough for anybody to get by on. You won't find this young woman going under so easily. The Wrights are a hardy family.' Just for a minute grey eyes met blue, the former cool and cynical. 'You don't feel like passing out, do you?'

'No,' she said. It was true. She had never felt less like passing out. Her pulse was racing still, but not entirely due to shock. No doubt Bryn was perfectly well aware of the effect his touch had on her. That would account for the satire. She pulled herself free of his light grasp and walked away from the three of them, trying not to limp. 'I'll throw you a towel out,' she called back over her shoulder.

Down in the cabin again she swiftly dried herself and got into the white dress, tying her hair up in a ponytail with the scarf she had worn earlier. She was sitting on one of the long cushions looking out of the porthole when Thea came down, and glanced round in surprise when the other picked up her hipsters and began to put them back on.

'We're going back to base,' proffered the American, sensing her scrutiny. 'There doesn't seem much point in going on.'

Tessa bit her lip. Thea didn't need to add that the ruination of the afternoon was entirely due to her; she already knew it. Bryn was doing this on purpose to bring home the point to her – as if he hadn't already done so. From the expression on Thea's face she wasn't in any mood to listen to any further apologies. Tessa made a helpless little gesture and turned back to the porthole again as the engine roared into life.

There was a pause before Thea said on a sudden

vicious note, 'You really are a prize brat, aren't you! No wonder Bryn is cheesed off! You've done nothing but follow him around since he got here.'

Tessa's head jerked. Had he said that? she wondered numbly. More important, did he believe it? From the moment when he had almost run Oliver down on the drive at Bay Marris Bryn had begun exerting the same irresistible pull she had known as a child, but she had imagined herself fairly successful in concealing it. Surely he couldn't imagine that she had engineered this whole mix-up today? That was ridiculous! Not even Val had known that the other two were going to be on board the boat when they got there.

'Bryn is only cheesed off because I'm trying to stop him buying Greenways,' she said with control. 'And I'm going to go on trying.'

'I thought the house belonged to your mother? Isn't she the one to say whether or not it's going to be sold?'

'Of course,' Tessa came back swiftly. 'But she doesn't *need* to sell it now, and that makes all the difference.'

'I see.' Comprehension was swift. 'Then it's true that she's going to marry Roland Wyman? Good for her! He's a real catch. One of the richest men on the island, I believe?'

Tessa looked at her with distaste. 'Is that your only measure of a good husband?'

'Not always.' A faint smile touched the red mouth. 'Just occasionally you find a man who could still make life pretty exciting even if he hadn't got a dime. Not that Bryn is ever likely to go broke. He has too many fingers in too many pies. You wouldn't know anything about that side of his life, I suppose?'

'No.' Tessa's brief flash of anger died an abrupt death. She wished Thea would go and leave her alone. She didn't think she could take much more. 'I think I'd like to lie down,' she said through stiff lips. 'I – I don't feel too good.'

'Shock, I expect.' To do her credit, Thea did not sound unsympathetic. 'I guess I'm not helping any by letting go at you this way, but you put Bryn's life in danger as well as your own. That was a rotten few minutes Val and I spent waiting for you both to come up.' She paused. 'Shall I send Val down?'

'No, thanks.' Tessa was fighting the nausea which kept coming over her in waves. 'I'd rather be on my own for a bit. It will pass off.'

Thea left her without saying anything else, and a moment later Tessa heard the faint sound of voices in the cockpit as she joined whoever was at the wheel. By keeping perfectly still she was able to control the nausea, and gradually it began to pass, although she still felt trembly and weak in the limbs. She didn't want to face Bryn again at all that day, only she didn't see how she was going to get out of it. Sick to death of her he might be, but ten to one he would consider himself partially responsible for the whole episode because he had been with her when it happened.

No one bothered her until they were once more tied up alongside the jetty back at the beach, and then to her relief it was Val who came down to fetch her, his concern all the more warming for its very lack of criticism.

Bryn was waiting with Thea on the jetty, dressed

once more in shorts and shirt. A brown and gold kerchief knotted at his throat gave his lean features an almost piratical air, further enhanced by the cynical expression on his face as he watched Val solicitously help her disembark.

'A small tot of brandy might not go amiss now that you're back on terra firma,' he said. 'How do you feel?'

'All right.' She made herself meet his eyes. 'I'm sorry I spoiled your afternoon.'

Something flickered in the greyness. 'It could have been worse. Maybe in future you'll follow the rules.' He seemed about to add something else, then apparently changed his mind. 'We'll get off. Be seeing you.'

'That brandy sounded a good idea,' Val remarked as they followed the other couple along the jetty. 'You still look pale.'

Tessa was watching the way Thea had taken Bryn's arm as they moved towards the palms, casual and easy as though she had done it a hundred times or more before, as she probably had. She swallowed on the constriction in her throat, said huskily, 'I think I'd just as soon have a cup of tea.'

'Fine, we'll both have one.'

They reached the villa as Bryn's car started up out front. Tessa sat on the veranda while Val went to see about the tea, and found herself listening exclusively to the receding sound of the engine, judging its direction. The nausea had gone by now, but it had left her with a dull, heavy ache behind the eyes. She made a determined effort to cheer herself up as Val came back to join her.

'It won't take long,' he said. 'Are you sure you don't want to lie down again for a while?'

'No, I'm fine now.' She smiled at him. 'I feel a bit of a fraud about the whole thing. After all, nothing very much happened.'

'No, but it could have done.' His face was serious. 'I suppose I should feel grateful to Bryn for getting you out of it, but I can't say that I approved of his tactics afterwards. Surely he must have realized that you aren't likely to forget an experience like that in a hurry?'

She shrugged, and tried to keep her voice light. 'I suppose it was a natural reaction. Anyway, he was right, I should have known better.' She added brightly, 'What do you usually do with your Sundays if it's six weeks since you even used the launch?'

'Oh, this and that. I can always find plenty to occupy my mind. I . . .' He broke off with a sudden dismissive little gesture as if he found the subject too trivial for further discussion, looked at her for a long moment, then said slowly, 'Tessa, I wonder if you realize just what I went through during those minutes while you were trapped down there? If anything had happened to you I think I would have . . .' Once again he cut the sentence, his colour deepening a fraction. 'I'm doing this all wrong – what my father would call "jumping the gun" – only I was never very good at waiting for anything. I realize we haven't known one another very long – as friends, I mean – but it's been long enough for me to know how I feel about you. I think I knew it the very first time Waldron introduced us. I – well, I suppose what I'm trying to say is that I want to marry you, Tessa – if you'll have me.'

She sat motionless looking at him, her eyes clouding. She felt lost for words, uncertain of how to handle a situation like this. She had realized that Val liked her a lot, and that his interest was showing signs of deepening, but not once had it entered her mind that he might actually be contemplating a more serious relationship just yet. They barely knew one another. Certainly not in the way two people should know one another before they got round to thinking about marriage. In any case, she didn't want to get married. Not to Val or ... anyone.

'You don't know what you're saying,' she managed at last. 'You can't decide you want to marry someone just because they nearly got themselves killed.'

'I didn't.' His smile was wry. 'I decided *that* quite some time ago. The only precipitate decision I'm guilty of is in telling you about it this way.' He dropped to a seat at her side on the cane settee, taking her cold hands in his. His face was set in almost pleading lines. 'Tessa, don't say no right away. Think about it. I've given you a surprise – I can see that now – but I really believed you'd already gathered how I felt about you. I mean, last night I . . .'

Tessa shook her head with sudden vigour. 'Last night you only talked about my coming to live here and the good times we'd have. The only time marriage was mentioned was in connection with my mother.' She paused, mouth tilting with a wry attempt at humour. 'It sounds like a Wyman take-over bid for the whole Wright family! Do you happen to have a young cousin tucked away somewhere who might do for Oliver one day?'

Val said a little stiffly, 'That's not very funny, Tessa.

I want to marry you for my sake, not because it happens to be convenient.'

'I know.' She put a penitent hand over his. 'I'm sorry, it's just that I couldn't think of anything else to say. I – I like you very much, and I've enjoyed being with you today, only . . . well, that's exactly it, isn't it? Today is the first time we've ever actually been together on our own, apart from the odd few minutes. Before it's always been in company. You've never even kissed me, or anything.'

'Not because I haven't wanted to. There hasn't been much opportunity up till now.'

'There was last night,' she reminded him softly, and closed her mind to the fleeting image of Bryn's taunting features out there on the beach. 'We were on our own then for quite some time.'

'Talking about the parents.' He was looking at her with a smile on his lips now. 'If that's all that's worrying you we can make up for lost time right here and now.'

Tessa made no move to withdraw as he pulled her closer to him. It wasn't by any means all that was worrying her, but something inside her needed to know what it would be like to be kissed by Val. She felt his lips move gently against her own, giving rather than demanding, heartwarming in their tender expression of an emotion she knew she couldn't begin to match. When he lifted his head again she hardly knew how to react. There had been none of the electric tingle Bryn had aroused in her the previous night, and yet she had not disliked it. Who could possibly dislike something so pleasant and . . . unassuming? She stared at him with a small frown unconsciously creasing the space between

112

her brows, until he reached out a finger and smoothed it away. His own expression was uncertain.

'Why don't you say something?' he asked. 'Was it so distasteful?'

'No, not at all.' Her reply was too quick, but he didn't seem to notice, his features relaxing a little.

'I'm glad. You haven't been kissed very often before, have you, Tessa?'

'No,' she said again truthfully, and wished she could think of some other remark to add to that flat statement of fact. Voice hesitant, she began, 'Val, I . . .'

'You don't have to explain anything.' His tone was understanding. 'You probably thought there would be more to it than that, even the first time. Well, there could have been, only I wanted you to know that I think the other aspects of love are just as important as the . . . physical side. Don't you?'

'I don't know. I mean, yes, I'm sure they are.' She was confused, and oddly depressed all of a sudden. 'Val, can't we just leave it as it is for the time being? I feel rather mixed up.'

'My fault. I did the whole thing the wrong way.' He sounded rueful. 'I should have settled for kissing you today and left the rest for a more suitable time. It isn't like me to get carried away like this, Tessa. I usually plan things very carefully.'

Tessa didn't doubt that for a moment. She supposed she should feel flattered that her little accident should have caused him to so far forget himself, but at the moment she couldn't work out how she felt about anything any more. A bare week ago she had been without a care in the world beyond finding enough hours in the day, whereas now . . .

'There's just one more matter I would like to mention,' Val said it carefully, as though feeling for the right way to put it. 'It was only last night that I realized how you feel about Greenways, but I do understand now that I've had time to think about it, so I want you to know that I'd be more than willing to buy the house myself, if you'd like it. It isn't very large now, admittedly, but it's in an excellent position with plenty of room to extend. In fact, I wouldn't mind living up there at all.'

It took Tessa a moment to clear her mind enough to take in the full sense of what Val was offering her. Her chest felt as if it had an iron band across it. If she married him she would be able to go on living in the home she had known and loved all these years, with the only difference being that her mother and Oliver would be down here on the coast. No, not the *only* difference, of course; she would also have a husband. Greenways meant a lot to her, she was ready to admit that. But did it really mean enough to consider marrying Val in order to stay there? If only she could sort out how she felt about him at all. He was so very nice, and considerate — not at all like Bryn who hadn't cared a whit about her feelings in the past, and thought nothing of them now either. *He* was only interested in getting his hands on Greenways. Once that purpose had been accomplished his whole reason for being in Barbados would have gone. It gave her a strange sensation to realize that she held the means of thwarting that purpose right here in her hands. All it would take was one little word . . .

The arrival of the tea-tray was perhaps a fortunate

diversion. By the time they were alone again the moment of temptation was past. She gave Val a small strained smile. 'Let's just go on being friends for the moment, can we?'

'All right.' He made every effort to conceal his disappointment. 'But you will promise to think about what I've said?'

Tessa made the promise, reflecting as she did so that it was going to be difficult to think about anything else. Instead of sorting themselves out her problems seemed to be multiplying, and they all related back to Bryn in one sense or another. That fact in itself held little comfort.

CHAPTER SIX

It was late when they got back to Greenways, but Roland was still there. Tessa only had to take one look at her mother's face to know that the question had been both asked and answered. She was grateful for the prior knowledge which enabled her to accept the news with appropriate responses, especially when she recognized the relief in the blue eyes so like her own. Roland had not been the only one, it seemed, to fear her reaction to the idea of a stepfather.

'I realize I can never take your own father's place,' he said to her quietly. 'And I shan't even try. I'd like it a great deal if you could come to look on me as you did on Waldron, though.'

It was only later, watching him talking with her mother, that Tessa realized for the first time how much like Waldron Marshall he was in manner, despite the difference in their ages. She wondered if her mother had noted it too.

At which point the celebration party for the four of them was first mentioned, Tessa was afterwards not quite sure, but before the Wymans eventually left at seven it had been arranged for the following evening. It was a relief to hear the cars move off. Tessa caught her mother's eye and hoped she sounded natural as she said, 'It turned out to be quite a week-end, didn't it?'

'It certainly did.' There was still a faint doubt in the gaze Shirley Wright rested on her daughter's face. 'Are you sure you're happy about Roland and me, Tessa? I mean, it's all been a bit of a surprise, even for me – although Roland did hint last night that he ...' She broke off, a smile hovering on her lips at some memory. 'Well, let's just say that I didn't expect a proposal the very next day. In a way I'm glad you didn't get round to asking Val about that job. At least—' there was a question in the quick glance – 'you didn't, did you?'

Tessa shook her head, aware that some of the shine might just disappear from her mother's eyes if she told the bare truth. There was no harm in concealing irrelevant detail. Roland had been going to ask her to marry him anyway. Impulsively she went and hugged her. 'I'm happy about it. Really and truly. Roland is great!' She turned away again a little to add on a lighter note, 'I can't see why you two should want Val and me with you tomorrow night. Wouldn't you rather go out on your own?'

Shirley laughed. 'We'll have plenty of time to be on our own. Anyway, it was Roland's idea to get the whole family together – apart from Oliver, of course. I'll have to ask Martha if she'll come in and stay with him. I can hardly farm him out after he's already spent the whole week-end with the St. Hills. I'm sure they'll have had more than enough of him by the time tomorrow morning comes round. You know what it's like getting him off to school on time.'

Tessa certainly did. She tried to imagine how he was going to react to the news, and came to the conclusion that for her young brother the fact that he would be living right beside the sea, with a beach, a boat *and* a swimming pool would more than outweigh any reservations regarding the acquisition of a new father. Oliver was nothing if not practical.

They were neither of them hungry enough to bother with a proper meal. Tessa made sandwiches, and left the coffee to perk while they ate them. When she came back from the kitchen again Bryn was sitting in the chair she had recently vacated. He greeted her casually without mentioning the afternoon at all, for which small mercy Tessa was grateful. She wondered what had happened to Thea. It was still only a little after eight-thirty, yet he had obviously been back some time, for he had changed from shorts and shirt into the beige suit he had worn that first night. The tautness was back inside her again. There was no need to ask why he had come; she already knew.

Her mother imparted her news over coffee, receiving his words of congratulation with a smiling shake of her head. 'Nothing ever takes you by surprise, Bryn. Have you trained yourself that way, or were you just born with it?'

He laughed. 'Maybe it just wasn't such a surprise in this case. I was there last night when Roland saw you arrive. When a man looks at a woman like that you can bet there'll be wedding bells in the not too far distant future. He's a lucky guy.'

'Thanks.' Shirley's voice was soft. 'I think I'm pretty lucky too. Of course, you realize this makes the decision over this place a great deal easier. Selling one's home because it's necessary is never very nice, but now that we'll all be moving down to the coast, Greenways isn't going to be any use to us anyway. I imagine that's why you came round tonight, isn't it?'

'One reason,' he admitted. His glance swung thoughtfully in Tessa's direction. 'Don't you have anything to say on the matter?'

'Yes, as a matter of fact, I do.' Her voice came out with amazing steadiness considering that she hadn't even planned what she was going to say. 'You're not the only one who wants Greenways. Val is thinking of buying it himself.'

'*Val* is?' Her mother had no reservations whatsoever about revealing *her* astonishment. 'When did he say that?'

Tessa caught her breath, suddenly aware that she couldn't tell the truth about this either without giving away the fact that Roland had told his son of his intentions before actually asking her if she would marry him. 'When we were out on the veranda before they left,' she improvised hastily.

'But why would Val want a house?' with bewilderment. 'Surely he doesn't imagine that I'll want him to leave his own home because I happen to be marrying his father?'

'I think the reason might be a little closer than that,' Bryn said levelly, but there was a certain constriction about his mouth. 'If Val wants to buy this place it's for Tessa, not himself.' The grey eyes claimed hers inexorably. 'Did you make it a condition?'

'What are you talking about? A condition to what?' Shirley looked from him to her daughter in some confusion. 'Tessa, you didn't ask Val to buy the house, did you?'

'No, he offered.' There was no way out of it; she was going to have to tell the truth now. Tessa fixed her gaze on a point midway between the two of them and tried to sound matter-of-fact. 'Val asked me to marry him this afternoon. Like father, like son, I suppose you could say.' She caught a glimpse of Bryn's face and hurried on, 'He knows how I feel about Greenways and he's willing to live here. As he says, there's plenty of room to extend.'

The silence seemed to stretch to infinity before anyone spoke, then her mother said slowly, 'Have you said you will marry him?'

'I said I'd think about it.' Her chin lifted a fraction. 'I *am* thinking about it. Aren't you pleased? You always said how much you liked Val.'

'I preferred him to the Summers boys as company for you. Marriage is something else entirely.' She hesitated. 'You're nowhere near old enough to be thinking about marrying anyone, Tessa.'

Her heart jerked. 'Plenty of girls get married at my age. I'll be twenty in a fortnight. And where could I find anyone more suitable than Val? He could have just about his choice out of the whole island.'

The other pair of blue eyes found those of the man sitting silently opposite, and her hands spread in a helpless little gesture. 'Did you ever get the feeling that you must have gone wrong somewhere but can't quite think how?'

'On odd occasions.' His tone was clipped. 'I think the best thing I can do is withdraw my offer for both house and land as of now, and leave you to sort things out between you.' He was getting to his feet as he spoke, his movements controlled but indicative of inner tension. The gaze he rested on Tessa made her flinch. 'Congratulations. You got your own way after all.'

He was gone before she could speak, had there been anything at all she could have said. She sat numbly in her chair, wishing with all her heart that she could have the previous few minutes over again. She might have won one victory, but in doing so she had forfeited every last atom of Bryn's friendship. He had known exactly what she was doing, and why. The worst part was that she had never meant to say what she had said at all. Seeing him sitting there, and knowing why he had come, had just brought the words tumbling from her lips without consideration.

'Tessa.' Her mother spoke quietly. 'Is it true what Bryn was implying, that you only threatened to marry Val in order to make him back out of buying Greenways?'

Was that the only reason? Tessa wondered in the fleeting moment before she forced herself to look up and across at her mother. It was the look on the latter's face which precipitated the second unconsidered decision in fifteen minutes. At that precise moment she wanted only to answer the plea for reassurance plainly visible in the well-loved features of her parent.

'The truth is that Val asked me to marry him *and* offered to buy Greenways,' she said. 'And I did promise to think about it. I know I was wrong to tell you about it the way I did – making it seem so calculated, I mean – but that's the way it came out. I wouldn't have spoken about it at all while Bryn was here, except that you were obviously ready to go and settle the deal with him right here and now.'

'Well, that's one aspect you're not going to have to

concern yourself over any more,' came the dry retort. 'I doubt very much if Bryn will show any further interest even if you decide not to marry Val after all.' That there was still some faint doubt left became apparent when she added, 'It's only a few days since you told me you found Val a bit of a bore.'

'That was because I was comparing him with Blake and Rob.' This, at least, Tessa could say with conviction. 'I realize now how unfair that was. Val has his own kind of life to lead, and he does it very well. I like him a lot.'

Her mother smiled a little. 'It isn't enough, Tessa. Not for marriage. You need to feel enough to get you through the rough bits as well as the smooth – and every marriage has some of both. If you'd ever been in love you'd know what I'm talking about.'

Something inside Tessa closed up tight. 'It doesn't always have to happen like a lightning shaft, though, does it?' she said roughly. 'You can fall in love quite slowly and gradually, can't you?'

'Of course. Providing you give yourself time. That's what I want you to do over Val. If he loves you enough he'll be willing to wait until you can return his feelings in the same way.' She paused. 'Roland has already said that what I do over this place is entirely up to me, so it wouldn't hurt to hang on to it, at least for a while. Give Val the first refusal in effect, although so far as I'm concerned I'd want you to have the house as a wedding present if things get that far.'

Tessa felt herself being drawn inexorably along like driftwood on the tide. Despite what her mother had said about needing some deeper emotion before contemplating marriage with Val, it was obvious that she found the idea itself pleasing enough. Probably Roland would too when he heard about it, which almost certainly wouldn't be long; father and son seemed to keep few secrets from one another. She thought of Val as he had been that afternoon, of the tender solicitude of his lips on hers. He should be very easy to love if she let herself think of him that way – if she *wanted* to think of him that way.

'Did you get around to deciding when your wedding is going to be?' she asked in an attempt to turn the focus of attention away from herself. 'I got the impression that Roland isn't going to wait very long.'

'No.' Her mother was smiling again, this time in a very different way. 'He suggested next week, but I persuaded him to wait the month out. We'd both like a quiet affair, with just family and close friends. Do you think we might get away with it?'

'There are going to be a lot of people feeling cheated if you do,' Tessa responded warmly. 'You know how everybody loves a wedding, and this isn't just anybody's wedding either. You'll be news.'

'I suppose we shall,' on a faintly wry note. 'You sound as though you'd quite look forward to it yourself. Have you any idea of the work entailed in organizing the kind of affair you're talking about in such a short time?'

Tessa could imagine. If she were totally honest, it was a part of her reason for suggesting it. To be involved in something up to her neck meant that much less time for dwelling on other matters, and at the moment that seemed a more than desirable state of affairs. 'We could do it,' she said, and managed to conjure up some semblance of her normal lighthearted tone. 'After all, as your only daughter I can bathe in reflected limelight.'

Shirley laughed. 'I suppose I should be thankful you're beginning to show an interest in such things! At one time I despaired that you'd ever really grow up, but now that you've begun you're certainly doing it fast. All right, I'll talk it over with Roland. I think he'll probably see it the same way when he thinks about it.' Her gaze went to the veranda door and clouded again for a moment. 'I only wish Bryn hadn't gone off the way he did. Even without Greenways he still has plenty of land for his purpose.' She gave a sigh. 'Anyway, I don't imagine we'll be seeing all that much of him from now on.'

Tessa didn't imagine so either, and the knowledge was like lead inside her.

The following week went by with surprising speed, urged on by the welter of preparations into which the two adult members of the Wright family found themselves suddenly plunged. As things turned out it was Roland himself who had brought up the matter of the size of the wedding over dinner on the Monday evening, reluctantly acknowledging the impossibility of limiting the guest list to any degree.

'Had you and Val been ready to name a day we might just have got away with it ourselves,' he said jestingly to Tessa when they had been left alone at the table at one point. He saw her change of expression and smiled. 'Yes, he told me he'd asked you, and I very much approve his choice, my dear, although I think he might have been wiser to bide his time a little longer. I gather you're not sure enough of your feelings yet.'

Tessa barely knew how to answer that one. 'I don't think I'm quite ready for marriage at all just yet,' she said at last. 'But I'm flattered that Val wants to marry me.'

'He's very much in love with you.' There was a pause, then he added softly, 'But that mustn't influence your decision, any more than his offer to buy Greenways for the two of you. Whatever happens you'll always have a home with us.'

Afterwards Tessa knew that was the moment when she finally accepted Roland into her affections. Not as any substitute for the father she had lost, but as a friend.

Oliver received the news of his mother's coming marriage in exactly the way Tessa had predicted, his initial caution giving way to wholehearted approbation on being introduced to his future home for the first time. Accustomed to a relatively quiet and orderly existence in a bachelor household, the staff were highly diverted by the coming changes, with the exception of Esma Layne who obviously saw her own position endangered. Once Shirley had tactfully made it clear that her services would still be required, however, the frost quickly thawed and Esma revealed herself more than eager to be involved in the wedding plans. It had already been decided that the reception would be held at the villa, Greenways being too small to accommodate everyone in comfort. Here, any overspill would have the whole stretch of terrace.

It was Roland who suggested a day at the races by

way of a break. The Barbados Turf Club held three meetings a year out at the Garrison Savannah, and they were one of the biggest draws on the island. Tessa had attended a couple in the past and enjoyed every exuberant minute. She found her spirits lifting to the idea of going again, especially when it meant being able to forget about guest lists and dress fittings and all the thousand and one other details for a whole day. Even Val agreed that it sounded an attractive proposition, despite the fact that it meant staying away from the store for once. He was making every effort to put her first, Tessa had to acknowledge, but at the back of her mind was the memory of Bryn's prediction on the night she had pushed him into the pool, cautioning her to wait and see how long the present state of affairs would last. True to her mother's prediction they had seen nothing at all of Bryn since the week-end. Tessa told herself it was better that way, and tried her hardest to believe it. There was no future in any other attitude.

The Garrison Savannah lies to the south of Bridgetown, wide and green, with the red brick buildings which once housed the British military still stretched along its perimeter. By the time the Wyman party arrived, the first race of the day had already been run, setting the meeting off to a good start with a win by the favourite. Everywhere was movement and colour, with the gaily-dressed crowds swarming between stalls and stands sprung up mushroom-like over the ground, the shouts of the vendors blending with the calypso rhythm of the band 'beating pan' by the grandstand. There was anticipation in the air, a festive spirit which gathered all comers. Tessa looked at Val with sparkling eyes.

'I'm going to have a bet on the next race. Come and help me choose a horse.'

'It's going to be impossible for us all to stay together,' stated Roland practically. 'We'll see the two of you back here at one o'clock for lunch.'

Val took Tessa's hand as they pressed through the crowd, keeping her close by his side. She risked a dollar on a mare called Match Maid because she felt sorry for it, calling Val a conservative when he backed the favourite himself.

Then they were off, to the cheers and screams of the spectators lining the rails, the jockeys' colours glinting in the sunlight as they urged on their mounts to greater efforts. Tessa leaned too far over the rail in excitement when somebody shouted that number three was gaining on the leader, and was only saved from finishing up on the track itself by the man standing next to her grabbing her by the shoulder and yanking her back again.

'Don' you go skinnin' no cuffins, little lady,' he grinned. 'That nummer three run like a lan' turkle!'

Tessa grinned back. 'Not this time!'

Round the corner by the clock and the field was into the straight, with two horses standing clear as they thundered into the last stretch up to the finishing line, first one and then the other forging slightly ahead until the light bay just managed that extra spurt which carried it triumphantly into the lead by a short head. Tessa gave a thumbs-up sign to her wry-faced neighbour before going to collect her winnings.

'Beginner's luck,' Val protested goodnaturedly when she crowed her delight. 'I bet that horse never wins another race in its life. What are you going to do with your extra dollar?'

'Frame it,' she returned, refusing to be put down. 'Maybe I just happen to have a natural eye for horseflesh. It isn't the first time I've bet on an outsider and won.'

He laughed. 'Well, if you never risk more than a dollar I suppose you can't go far wrong. What would you like to do now?'

'Oh, just look round. There's always so much to see.' She was pivoting as she spoke, heading into the milling throng so that Val was forced to follow in order to keep her in sight. 'I'm glad Oliver went to school,' she said over her shoulder, 'or we'd have spent the whole morning looking for him.' Her eyes fell on a man coming away from a nearby stall with a golden brown pork chop held sizzling to his lips, a chunk of home-made bread held ready in his other hand to catch the drips already running down his chin. 'I'd love one of those!'

Val looked at her as if she had suddenly sprouted horns. 'You're not serious?'

'Of course.' She was genuinely surprised. 'They do them at every meeting. They're delicious! Wouldn't you like one too?'

He shook his head. 'It's hardly wise.' He didn't need to add that he hardly considered it seemly either. 'They've probably been standing in the sun all morning. Anyway, hygiene is never very thorough in these places. You don't know what you might pick up.'

Tessa supposed he was right, but it took a lot out of the day to see it that way. What if you did pick up a few germs here and there? It was all part and parcel of the enjoyment. Just for a moment she yearned for Blake and the others. Last year they had sampled just about everything there was to sample, and none of them had suffered any ill-effects. Something to do with mind over matter, perhaps. She didn't know. All she did know was that she had enjoyed her last race meeting a great deal more than she was beginning to enjoy this one.

She was almost glad when the time came to rejoin the parents. She was a little ahead of Val as they emerged from the thick of the crowd at the point where they had agreed to meet up again, and she felt her heart lurch at the sight of the couple standing with Roland and her mother. It was odd, but she somehow hadn't considered the possibility of meeting Bryn here, and yet it should have been more than apparent that the chance was there. She nerved herself to show no sign of her inner tension as she moved towards the group, suddenly glad of Val at her back.

'Hallo, you two,' smiled Roland. 'Had a good time?'

'Great.' Tessa had no intention of letting any of them think otherwise. 'I backed the winner in the second race.'

'Match Maid?' Bryn's tone was pleasant if impersonal. 'You must have second sight. It's never done much before.'

'It didn't have Tessa rooting for it. We'll have to put her in touch with the trainer.' Thea was smiling, but there was a certain malicious glint in her eyes. She was wearing a simply cut dress in amber wild silk which made Tessa feel like a country cousin in her plain blue linen.

'I've invited these two to join us for lunch,' said Roland. 'Unfortunately they've already made other arrangements.'

'Such a shame.' Thea didn't sound quite as regretful as her words implied. 'It would be nice another time, perhaps.' She took a rather pointed glance at her watch. 'Bryn, we really should be on our way.'

'Yes.' It was impossible to tell what he was thinking from his expression. 'Perhaps you'd all like to be *my* guests for dinner this coming Saturday? It's time the house had a proper airing.'

Tessa said without thinking, 'Will Josh be able to manage?' and drew a faint smile.

'He won't have to. I've extended the staff to three. You can come with an easy mind.'

She could go; it certainly would not be with an easy mind. Tessa listened to Roland accepting for them all and wondered what excuse she could possibly conjure up to get out of it. If Thea was going to be there, and it was very unlikely that she would not be, then she didn't want to be. Seeing her playing hostess at Bay Marris would be more than she could bear.

The rest of the afternoon was something of an anticlimax. Even Roland was moved to remark that it might have been a better idea to visit the races in the afternoon instead of the morning, it apparently not having occurred to him that a lot of people found enough entertainment there for a whole day.

Tessa swam in the pool with Val after lunch, and spent a lazy hour or so on one of the loungers pretending to be asleep so that she wouldn't be called on to talk. She knew she wasn't being fair to Val in not telling him the truth with regard to her feelings. She could never marry him, not in a million years. Seeing Bryn again had convinced her of that. It seemed advisable, however, to let the matter rest for now, at least until after the wedding. Only deep down would she admit that she was only putting off the inevitable.

Oliver was to be picked up from school and brought down to the villa for the rest of the afternoon and evening. He arrived looking rather pale and sorry for himself, with a message from his teacher to the effect that he had begun feeling sick soon after lunch. It was indicative of just how bad he felt when he made no demur to Roland's suggestion that he be put to bed. His mother went with him, and stayed until he finally fell asleep, returning to the veranda with a small frown creasing her brow.

'I hope he isn't coming down with anything,' she said. 'So far we've managed to avoid most of the usual childhood illnesses.'

'I believe children often get these feverish attacks without them coming to anything,' Roland reassured her. 'It might be a good idea if he stayed where he is for the time being, however, just in case. There's no reason why you shouldn't all spend the night here, if it comes to that.'

'We don't have anything with us,' Tessa put in quickly. 'And there's Oliver's menagerie to be fed and watered. We can't leave them all night.'

'That's no problem,' Val interposed before her mother could comment. 'I can run you up to Greenways after dinner and do all that's necessary. We'd be back for ten.'

His father nodded. 'That's settled, then. I'll get Esma to see to your rooms.' He smiled in Tessa's direction.

'Val thought you'd probably prefer a view of the sea. You can see what you think of it tonight. If you like the room he chose for you then it will be yours from now on.'

Tessa's responding smile felt strained. She only hoped it didn't show. It was silly to feel the way she did about spending the night here, but she couldn't help it. Compared with this Greenways might be small, even shabby, but it was home in a way the villa could never be. Not to her. She felt she wanted to spend as much time in that home as she could before the wedding.

Oliver was still feeling too ill to be moved at dinner time. Tessa and Val left soon afterwards, reaching Greenways in half an hour. It felt strange to be in the house at night with only Val for company. Tessa went and packed the items her mother had asked for in a small grip, then moved through to her own room to complete her task.

Only then did she acknowledge that she had no real intention of returning with Val that night. There was no need for her to return. In any case, someone should stay and keep an eye on things here.

He looked round from the veranda doors as she came back to the living room carrying the bag. 'All ready?'

'I'm not coming.' She said it a little more abruptly than she had intended and hastened to add, 'It seems silly coming all that way back just for one night. Anyway, I don't like leaving the house empty. Martha will be here at seven and she'd wonder what on earth had happened.'

'You could always leave her a note.' Val's smile had disappeared. 'Tessa, I can't leave you here alone. What do you think your mother is going to say if I turn up without you?'

'I daresay she'll think I'm old enough to spend one night without a guardian,' she returned with some asperity. 'Don't fuss, Val. I'll be perfectly all right.'

He hesitated, the uncertainty plainly written on his face. 'I'm sure if we phone her and ask she'll say you're to come back with me.'

'Then we won't do it.' Tessa was determined to have her own way. 'I'll make us some coffee, and then you'd better get off. I'll phone in the morning to see how Oliver is, although as your father said it's probably just a bilious attack.' She softened a little at his troubled expression. 'Val, it's only one night, and I do think someone should be here. I'll lock all the doors as soon as you've gone. Honestly.'

His smile was wry. 'I suppose if you've made up your mind there isn't a great deal I can do about it. Don't bother with the coffee, though. It's getting late, and your mother will be waiting for these.'

He gave her a gentle kiss before going out, standing on the veranda until she had closed and locked the doors, then lifting a hand in reluctant farewell. Tessa stood there until the sound of the engine had faded into the night, her eyes scanning the familiar room lit by the soft glow of a solitary lamp. Now that she was alone as she had planned she was forced to acknowledge a certain jumpiness, an inclination to probe the shadowed corners. It was ridiculous, of course. There had been no one in the house when they arrived, and certainly no opportunity for anyone to have crept in while they'd been here. Apart from that, it was she who had wanted to stay, and if it now seemed not quite such a good idea then it was entirely her own fault and she would have to make the best of things.

She made some coffee and drank it in the living room with the blinds drawn against the night. Val would be back at the villa by now, she calculated after half an hour had passed. Any moment she expected the telephone to ring – or was it *hoped* the telephone would ring? But it didn't, and she had no intention of giving herself away by ringing them!

The coffee had long since gone cold when she finally nerved herself to go to bed. She undressed swiftly, contenting herself with a brisk splash and a teeth clean before sliding between the sheets, then lying there rigidly listening to the night sounds and recalling the stories Martha had told her about the 'duppies' which floated around by night scaring honest folk out of their wits. But such creatures only inhabited the air outside, didn't they? Within four walls it was as safe as houses.

Tessa gave an involuntary little chuckle and felt her limbs relax as common sense overtook primitive fear. Honestly, anyone would think she was about twelve instead of almost twenty! There were no such things as duppies, or any other kind of spirit creatures, if it came to that. It was all in the imagination.

She was drifting, almost asleep, when the faint sound of a door closing somewhere in the house brought her instantly and heart-thumpingly awake. Footsteps came softly along the corridor in the direction of her room, pausing outside her door as she came jerking upright in stark terror, the hair at the back of her head literally lifting. She wanted to scream, but no sound would come. And who was there to hear her?

The rap on the wood and Bryn's voice saying her name brought a relief so great she momentarily felt sick. It was all she could do to stop herself from leaping from the bed and rushing out to the safety of his arms.

'I'm in bed,' she called weakly, and then as full realization dawned, she added on a stronger note, 'What on earth are you doing here in the middle of the night?'

He came into the room before answering, switching on a lamp to eye her unsmilingly. 'Who did you think I was?' he asked. 'I could feel the vibrations through the door!'

The jeer brought a stab of resentment. What did he expect? People had been known to die of fright before this. She made a valiant attempt to gain control of the situation. 'Never mind who I thought you were. How did you get in?'

'Through the side door. It wasn't locked.' He was leaning against the jamb in a characteristic pose, hands jammed into the pockets of his slacks. He was wearing a cotton shirt, open at the neck, and his hair was ruffled as though he had only recently pulled on the latter. A pair of espadrilles completed his attire. 'Your mother has been trying to reach you by phone for the last couple of hours,' he went on. 'Apparently your line is out of order. Finally she phoned through to Bay Marris and asked me to check on you. What's the idea of spending the night there on your own?'

Tessa gathered the sheet a little more closely about her, not caring for his mood. 'I didn't want to leave the place empty. I'm sorry you've been bothered, but as you can see I'm perfectly all right. What time is it?'

'About twelve-thirty,' he said without bothering to look at his watch. He came away from the door-jamb and crossed to the bed, picking up the cotton housecoat she had thrown there and tossing it towards her. 'Put that on and get a few things together. I told your mother I'd take you back to Bay Marris with me.'

'Did you!' She was suddenly and furiously angry. 'Well, you can go back and tell her I wouldn't come. I'm staying right here!'

'No, you're not.' It was said without change or rise of tone, but the familiar inflexible line had crept into the set of his mouth. 'I said I'd fetch you back and that's exactly what I'm going to do. Are you going to get out of bed under your own steam, or shall I get you out?'

She gazed at him for what seemed like an age, heart beating fast and hard. He meant it. What she wanted had no bearing on the situation. To be fair it wasn't the actual *going* over to Bay Marris which bothered her so much; after the fright she had undergone she would be lucky to get off to sleep again if he did leave her alone. What did rankle was the way in which he simply took it for granted that she would do as she was told, like some kid Oliver's age. She tried another tack, aware that she was only prolonging the inevitable and wondering why she bothered.

'Bryn, it really isn't necessary to go to all this trouble.' Her voice was quieter now and reasonable. 'It's time I learned to be independent.'

He snorted derisively. 'Since when were you *not* independent. Even at fourteen you pleased yourself before thinking of others. Your mother doesn't like the idea of you sleeping on your own, and that's good enough for me. If Val had any sense he'd have packed you into the car. He must have realized how your mother was likely to react.'

'I suppose he did, but unlike you Val credits me with a mind of my own.'

'You mean he gives in too easily. God help him if he does marry you!' The last on a biting note. 'I'll wait out on the porch. Don't bother to dress. It's hardly worth it.'

Tessa slid her feet to the floor as the door closed behind him. That last jibe had stung in a way which went a lot deeper than the actual words. So far as Bryn was concerned the possibility of her marriage to Val mean nothing beyond the fact that it had lost him the chance of buying Greenways. She only wished she could school herself to feel the same indifference over his relationship with Thea Ralston.

Despite what he had said about not getting dressed, she dragged on a pair of jeans and a shirt before going out to join him. He took the duffle bag containing her night things from her without a word, and personally supervised the locking of the door before heading across the grass to the path.

'I've forgotten to leave a note for Martha,' Tessa exclaimed, pausing in her tracks as they reached the hedge.

'I did it while you were getting ready,' he said.

'Oh.' She started moving again, aware of an irrational annoyance. 'You think of everything, don't you?'

He glanced her way, mouth curving without humour. 'I try.'

137

There was nothing else said all the way over to the house. They went in by way of the library, reminding Tessa of the last time Bryn had brought her to Bay Marris in the night. It seemed a long time ago now. He went straight over to the desk to lift the telephone receiver and dial a number.

The call was answered right away, indicating that the recipient must have been sitting by waiting for it. Bryn spoke briefly but succinctly, then held the instrument out to Tessa.

'Your mother wants to speak to you.'

The familiar voice sounded distorted over the crackling wire. 'You shouldn't have sent Val back without you, Tessa. You knew I'd be worried about you being up there on your own. He was most upset when we found the line out of order. Have you any idea of the trouble you've caused?'

'I think so.' Tessa was conscious that Bryn could probably hear both sides of the conversation from where he was standing. 'I'm sorry. I should have realized.'

'Yes, you should. I hope you've apologized to Bryn too. I didn't like the idea of getting him out at this time of night, but I couldn't think of anything else, apart from having Val come back in the car.' There was a pause. When she spoke again the sharpness had diminished. 'Well, at least I'll be able to sleep myself knowing that you're over at Bay Marris. Oliver seems a bit better; his temperature is down. All being well we should be home before lunch.'

Bryn was lighting a cheroot when she turned round after ringing off. 'Why don't you sit down for a bit?' he said. 'Your room should be ready, but we'll give it another minute or two to be sure.'

Tessa took one of the easy chairs, perching uncomfortably on the edge of the cushion. 'What will your new staff think to you bringing back a guest at this hour?' she asked on a deliberately flippant note.

'Not much,' came the dry return. 'My housekeeper is what you might call outspoken.'

'A housekeeper?' She tried to keep her voice casual. 'Does that mean you're planning to stay longer than you anticipated?'

'Not necessarily. Without Greenways I'm having to revise my plans all round – pull in my oars. But whatever happens the place will need looking after.'

It was a moment before she could bring herself to say, 'I suppose I'm to blame for ruining everything this way for you.'

'You're to blame for a whole lot more than you seem to realize.' He wasn't looking at her but at the glowing end of the cheroot, mouth cynical. 'Old grudges take a long time dying. If I'd realized what I was going to get into I'd have stayed away another five years. You'd probably have been a married woman by then – though not to Val Wyman.'

'Why not to Val?'

'You're not in love with him. At least, you certainly weren't the last time we talked, and you don't fall in love in a few days.'

Didn't you, though? thought Tessa numbly. She was in a position to refute that statement right now, but she couldn't take advantage of the opportunity. Being in love with Bryn was her misfortune; he certainly hadn't encouraged her.

'It isn't absolutely necessary to be in love to make a marriage work,' she said to break the silence. 'In some countries it's regarded as the last consideration.'

'We're not talking about other places. And you're neither old enough or jaded enough to think that way yourself. Val might be in a position to give you all the things you're obviously starting to crave for, but it's going to take more than that to make you happy.'

She stole a glance at him. 'I didn't think my happiness concerned you very much.'

'No?' He sounded suddenly savage. 'Considering that I seem to have spent most of the time I've known you trying to keep you out of trouble of one kind or another that's a bit of a sweeping statement. All right, maybe I handled you the wrong way five years ago, but how long do I have to go on paying for it?'

Tessa felt her cheeks warm. 'I don't know what you're talking about.'

'Oh, come on.' He made an impatient movement. 'Credit me with a little sense. We had an awkward relationship and I failed to make the grade. You were such a bundle of contradictions it's small wonder I did fail! How would you have had me deal with a situation like that?'

It would be childish, she decided, to further deny any knowledge of the situation he was referring to. 'Not with mockery,' she retorted. 'You could have just ignored it.'

He gazed at her for a moment, expression ironical. 'Sure I could. You made it easy to ignore. Fourteen you may have been, but you were advanced enough to make that fact a bit difficult to remember on occasion. Teasing you was my defence against other instincts. How do you think you'd have reacted if I'd kissed you the way you used to ask to be kissed?'

'I didn't act like that at all!' She was half embarrassed, half indignant. 'I might have thought you were the bee's knees for a time, but that was as far as it went.'

'Oh, I'm not saying you knew exactly what you were doing. It's probably instinctive in the female to look at the male the way you used to look at me. I've even seen a five-year-old do it.' He shook his head wryly. 'Believe me, I exercised considerable restraint where you were concerned!'

She was silent for a long moment, almost unable to believe what he was saying, except that it had a ring of truth about it.

'If you hadn't I might have got over it a whole lot quicker,' she ventured at last.

'But I wouldn't.' His voice was suddenly softer. 'As it is, I've spent five years waiting for you to grow up enough for me to risk coming back, only to find you hating my guts still. Maybe I just expected things to be different this time.'

Tessa stared up at him from the depths of the chair, eyes huge and dark. 'Don't tease me, Bryn,' she got out.

'I'm not trying to.' He put down the cheroot and came across to where she sat, pulling her up out of the chair and holding her in front of him so that she had to look at him. There was no mockery in the grey eyes now. 'You're still the same tantalizing little wretch I left behind, but at least you're old enough to be dealt with as a woman. You're not going to marry Val Wyman, Tessa, and you're going to tell him so tomorrow. After that we can perhaps start getting to know one another over again – properly this time. Agreed?'

The knot had begun to uncurl, but cautiously. 'Bryn—' she began, and felt his finger come over her lips, cutting off what she had been about to say. He was smiling.

'No arguments. You've already admitted that you don't love Val, so there's no problem. And if this will add any weight to my side of it . . .'

Tessa felt her last doubts crumble under the pressure of his mouth on hers. He meant it. He really meant it! She went into his arms without reservation, thrilling to the warm, confident strength of him, looking at him with bright eyes and flushed cheeks when he finally held her away from him.

'Unpredictable as ever,' he smiled. 'Are we going to stop fighting after this?'

She smiled back. 'Over Greenways? I imagine so. As you once pointed out, I can hardly live there on my own, and if I'm not going to marry Val I don't think he'll have much interest in buying it.' Her face clouded. 'How am I going to tell him?'

'That's something you're going to have to work out for yourself. It isn't as if you'd actually accepted him yet.'

'Yes, I know, but it still isn't going to be easy.'

'Easy or not it has to be done. And right away. By rights I shouldn't even be kissing you, I suppose, until you've straightened things out with him, but that kind of forbearance is a little beyond me.'

He kissed her again with satisfying thoroughness, then reluctantly let her go. 'Time you were in bed, I think. You've got the room next to mine, so don't walk in your sleep.'

'I won't.' She wanted badly to stay with him a little longer, but did not yet feel confident enough to demur. In any case, she needed time to think, time to take in the full joyous implications of all that he had said to her tonight. Bryn had stayed away from Barbados because of her, because he had been waiting for her to grow up. She felt all of that right now.

The housekeeper met them at the head of the stairs. She must have weighed all of sixteen stones but carried it so well that even in the gaudily flowered wrap which covered her ample frame she managed to retain a certain dignity.

'Everythin' all ready,' she announced. 'Ah put she in room that yuh said. Yuh min' me gettin' along muh own bed agin now?'

'No, that's fine.' Bryn accepted the apparent belligerence of the question without batting an eyelid. 'Thank you, Ambrosine.'

'And I'm sorry to have got you up at this time of night,' ventured Tessa.

'Sure nuff a mighty funny time to come visitin',' muttered the housekeeper as she turned her bulk back along the landing.

Bryn was smiling. 'Her bark's worse than her bite. Josh recommended her.' He was pushing open the door of the room indicated as he spoke, ushering Tessa inside. 'You'll be all right in here. Have you got everything you need?'

Tessa nodded without speaking, wanting him to kiss her again, yet suddenly almost shy of him. But he made no attempt to take her in his arms, merely slid a hand gently round the back of her neck beneath the fall of hair and held her like that for a moment studying her, a smile curving his lips. Then he let her go.

'Pleasant dreams,' he said. 'I'll see you in the morning.'

CHAPTER SEVEN

TESSA awoke at seven to full recollection of the previous night's events. She lay where she was for a few moments, looking round the lovely blue and white guest room with its period furnishings and tray ceiling. She had always wanted to sleep in the fourposter bed, but hardly felt in the mood to appreciate it properly right now. If Bryn was still in his room he was only the bare thickness of a wall away; he would hear her if she called his name. She wasn't going to, of course, but it was a wonderful feeling all the same.

Unable to stand inaction any longer, she got up, crossing to the window to lean out and take a deep breath of the fragrant morning air. This room looked out on the side of the house. Only by leaning right over could she get a glimpse of the pool through the trees, and it was impossible to tell whether anyone was down there yet. She could hardly wait to see Bryn again, and yet there was a particular kind of delight in just thinking about him too, contemplating the time they were going to spend together getting to know one another in the way he had said.

A cloud came down over that delight as she recalled the task she must perform today. Telling Val she couldn't marry him would not be pleasant, especially when it was only a few days since she had intimated that time might be all she needed. One thing she must do was to keep Bryn right out of it. What was between them was too new and too precious to be paraded just yet. And she supposed that what he had said last night was also true. Until she had straightened things out with Val once and for all he was not in any position to further his own claims. There was a momentary doubt there, quickly overcome by the recollection of his kisses. Of course Bryn's attentions were serious. He would hardly have talked the way he had if they hadn't been. It was still difficult to imagine the way he had felt about her before. No wonder he had left the island so abruptly. It spoke volumes for his basic integrity.

Despite her haste last night, habit had caused her to stuff a swimsuit into her bag along with her night clothes. She could hear Joshua's voice from the rear of the house as she went downstairs, and another voice answering him. That would be Ambrosine Spencer. Tessa smiled to herself. Somehow the name suited the woman despite its fancy sound. And if Josh had recommended her then Bay Marris had found itself a fitting housekeeper especially as Bryn would not be leaving quite so soon now.

It was something of a disappointment to find the pool empty. Tessa had been in the water several minutes before she saw Bryn coming down from the house. He was wearing a short towelling robe – reminding her that she still had the one he had loaned her the other night. He smiled when he saw her, and lifted a hand in greeting before stripping off the robe to dive in.

'Hi there,' he said softly a moment later, treading water at her side. 'Sleep well?'

'Yes.' Once again Tessa felt the unfamiliar shyness come over her, the mingling of anticipation and reticence at his closeness. 'I've always liked that room.'

'You have?' There was a taunting glint in his eyes, but for once it failed to jar. His hair gleamed with moisture in the bright light, dripping down into his neck. He ran a hand over it, smoothing the crisp thickness to his head for a brief moment before it sprang to life again. Then he took Tessa by the elbows, drawing her effortlessly towards him and keeping them both afloat with the movements of his legs as he kissed her lightly on the lips.

'Come on out,' he said. 'I can't kiss you properly in here.'

She said breathlessly, 'What about your swim?' and saw him smile.

'I can manage without.'

He gave her a hand up the steps, gathering her to him the moment she reached the edge. This time the kiss lasted longer. Tessa made no demur. So far as she was concerned it could go on for ever. When he did let her go her shyness had flown. She was able to meet his eyes with confidence, uncaring of what he must read in her own. She wished this thing with Val was already settled so that nothing stood between them. Being with Bryn like this was all she had dreamed of: tender; compassionate, yet with a hint of demands to come which both scared and thrilled her. For the moment he was holding back, mindful, perhaps, of her lack of experience. She loved him the more for it. With a man like Bryn there was no limit to emotion; it would grow and keep on growing in her.

'When are you seeing Val?' he demanded, echoing her thoughts. 'Will he be coming out here, or are you expected there?'

'Mom said she and Oliver would be home for lunch if Oliver was well enough to travel. Val may bring them.' She hesitated. 'Is it so important that I tell him today, Bryn?'

'Yes.' He was gentle but emphatic. 'You'd better phone through and make sure he does come with your mother. Then we can get everything straightened out.' He gave her a smile which made her pulses leap. 'I want to know exactly where I am.'

Did he intend to make his own feelings clear to everyone too? she wondered. That would hardly be tactful if Val were still around. On the other hand, he perhaps considered it kinder in the long run. If Val knew about it he would not harbour any false hopes of changing her mind.

'I'll phone right after breakfast,' she said. 'He never leaves for the Store before nine.' She laughed with sudden sheer exuberance. 'I'm starving! Race you back to the house!'

She heard Bryn laugh as he caught her up half-way across the grass between the trees, then he was swinging her up into his arms, holding her there to look into her upturned face.

'You don't get away that easily,' he said. 'I always could catch you. How about paying the forfeit?'

She did so, marvelling at her newfound ability to play such games. He put her lightly back on her feet and they went the rest of the way together, his arm about her shoulders. Only when they reached the house did they part to go and get changed. Tessa sang as she did so.

They had breakfast out on the veranda, although

Tessa found herself too churned up inside to eat. Bryn seemed troubled by no such emotional drain on his appetite. She watched him demolish a plate of ham and eggs and wondered at the constitution which could face such a meal at this time of the morning in a temperature already climbing into the upper seventies.

The telephone rang while he was still only half-way through. Joshua came out to tell Tessa that her mother was on the line.

She took the call in the library just along the veranda from where they were sitting. Oliver was as right as rain this morning, Shirley Wright informed her. In fact, he was fit enough for school. Roland had suggested that they take advantage of her being at the villa to finalise arrangements for the reception, so it would be lunch-time before she got home.

'Why don't you stay and have lunch down there?' suggested Tessa quickly. 'I can always have that cold chicken and salad left over from Wednesday.'

'Well, I suppose it might not be a bad idea.' It was obvious from her tone that she found it a very tempting idea. She paused. 'I'm afraid Val isn't here right now. He was called to the Store about twenty minutes ago. Some minor crisis or other, nothing to worry about, he said. He's going to phone you later on.'

The reprieve was only temporary, but Tessa was glad of it. She said a lighthearted goodbye to her mother, and went back to tell Bryn the news.

'I was thinking,' she tagged on diffidently, 'that it might not be a bad idea to wait until tomorrow when we all come here to dinner to talk to Val. It isn't as if I were engaged to him, or anything.'

149

The shake of Bryn's head was decisive. 'I don't agree. It isn't fair to let him go on thinking you're going to marry him any longer than strictly necessary. By the time you all come here I want to know that Val is fully aware of his standing with you.' He looked at her for a moment, tone softening. 'If not for his sake then for mine, Tess.'

He was right, and she knew it. She sighed and gave in. 'All right, when he phones I'll tell him I want to see him tonight. I'm afraid Roland is going to be disappointed. He was quite keen on the idea.'

'Well, he can't have everything. Anyway—' with a faint grin – 'one Wright is quite enough in a family. As it is he'll have Oliver to contend with as an extra, although I can't imagine he's going to be as much of a problem as his sister was.' He stretched, and pushed back his chair. 'I'll take that swim a bit later on. Want to join me?'

Tessa didn't much mind what they did. So long as she could be with him she was happy.

They swam about ten-thirty, afterwards stretching out on a couple of loungers at the poolside to dry off. Bryn did most of the talking, answering her questions about his life during the last five years in tolerant detail. Where his job was concerned, Tessa already knew that he was at the top; able to pick and choose his contracts almost anywhere in the world. She wanted to ask him where he would be off to next, but that would be bringing the future too much into focus. For the time being she was content to contemplate only the present.

The mention of Brazil caused her to say casually, 'It's odd that no one's seen anything of Eric Varley since the party. Val said his boat was gone from the Wharf.' She paused. 'You never did tell me about him.'

'I never intended to,' he returned. 'I don't know what he was doing in Barbados, and I don't want to know, but whatever it was you can bet your last dollar he was up to no good.'

'But if you've never met him before—'

'I was once shown his photograph.'

'Oh.' She digested that in silence for a moment, her brows drawing together. 'Who showed it to you?'

His sigh held resignation. 'You're not going to rest till you've got it all are you? If you must know it was a woman who once had an affair with him. She was on the verge of leaving her husband for him when he took off. She asked me if I'd ever met up with him.'

'Is that all?'

'Isn't it enough?' He glanced at her, then shrugged. 'No, it isn't all. I've heard his name mentioned in various places since then. There are quite a few people interested in catching up with Eric Varley for various reasons, any one of which was more than adequate reason for getting you out of his clutches that night at the party. I can't personally prove anything against him, but he certainly wasn't fit company for a young innocent like you.'

'Is that how I still seem to you?' she ventured, and felt his hand come over to push lightly at her chin.

'I think you'll be a quick learner with the right teacher, but there's no rush.' His tone was suddenly a little rough. 'I'll be glad when you've had that birthday.'

'Does that mean you'd rather I'd been older?'

'In one way I suppose it does. A twelve-year age gap

takes some bridging.' He smiled faintly. 'Makes me feel I'm taking an unfair advantage.'

Josh arrived to tell Bryn he was wanted on the phone before Tessa could formulate an adequate reply to that latter statement. When he returned some few minutes later he was wearing a rueful expression.

'I'm afraid I'm going to have to go out. Something cropped up. Will you stay on here till I get back?'

'Of course.' She tried hard not to let her disappointment overshadow the whole day. It must be important or he wouldn't be going. She would have liked to know more about it, but Bryn didn't seem disposed to tell her any more than he already had, and she couldn't bring herself to ask. 'What time will you be back?' she said instead.

'As soon as I can. I've told Ambrosine you'll be staying for lunch, though I may not make it myself.' He smiled and put a hand briefly to her cheek. 'Behave yourself.'

She watched him through the trees, wishing he had kissed her good-bye. Maybe he thought they'd done enough kissing for one morning. She smiled to herself at that. Nineteen, twenty, or any other age, she would never have had enough. Not where Bryn was concerned. The touch of his lips, the feel of his arms about her – it was all too wonderful for words. Just being with him at all was a delight. She didn't know how she was going to get through the next couple of hours or so until he got back.

It seemed a good idea to take the opportunity while he was gone to slip across home and put on something a little more feminine against his return. Tessa went back to the house when she heard the car leave, and gathered her things together, then walked over to Greenways.

Martha was on the point of leaving when she got there, although she would normally have stayed until one o'clock.

'I've got a beatin' in the head,' she explained, pressing both hands to her crown to add emphasis to her claim. 'I ninted mahself with some stuff yuh got in the cupboard, but it don't seem to have done no good. I been waitin' on yuh to come.'

'Oh, I'm sorry!' Tessa was immediately contrite. Martha was no malingerer. 'Would you like me to run you down home in the car?'

'I'd rather walk. Don' want no bad feels in mah stomach. I'll see yuh tomorrow, God spare life.' Half-way to the door she turned to add 'They done been fix the phone.'

No doubt Roland's doing, Tessa reflected. Last time they had waited a week before anyone came out to see to the fault. Having a man around to speak for them certainly made a difference.

She was pulling on the blue dress she had worn that first evening with Bryn when the telephone rang. Tugging the skirt hastily into place, she went through to the living room to answer it. Val sounded a little cool.

'I've been waiting for you to give me a ring,' he said. 'I just tried Bay Marris and they said you were over at your place.' He paused briefly. 'I understand you spent the night there.'

'Yes, but it wasn't exactly my suggestion.' Tessa was defensive and somewhat resentful. 'I wasn't to know the phone was out of order. If I'd been able to speak to

Mom myself she wouldn't have needed to get in touch with Bryn at all.'

'If you'd agreed to come back with me it wouldn't have mattered anyway,' he pointed out with unanswerable logic. 'I think you were a bit inconsiderate all round, Tessa. After all, if we're going to be married I have a right to expect—'

'That hasn't been settled yet, has it?' It was Tessa's turn to be cool. Then she caught herself up. It was neither fair nor right to broach the subject over the telephone. She had to tell him her decision to his face. 'Val,' she said hesitantly, 'I don't want to quarrel with you. Can we talk about it tonight?'

'I'm afraid I'm tied up tonight.' He sounded perturbed. 'I'm free now, though, till two. Could you come down to town and have lunch with me?'

It took her only a moment to make up her mind. The sooner she got it over with the better, even if it did mean not being here when Bryn got back. When she did see the latter again she would be in a position to tell him that everything was sorted out.

'All right,' she agreed. 'Shall I come to the Store?'

'Yes, do that. I'll be in my office. Anyone will direct you.' His voice took on a certain urgency. 'Tessa—'

'See you in about half an hour,' she said, and hung up.

She was ready to leave in five minutes, but first there was a phone call to Bay Marris to tell Ambrosine that she would not after all be taking lunch there, and to leave a message for Bryn stating simply that she had gone to see Val. He would understand. She might even be back before him. It was unlikely that Val would want to linger over their meal once she had said what she had to say to him.

For its age the Morris was a good runner and usually reliable, providing one remembered to pander to its needs now and then. Tessa rarely did remember to top up the radiator, and could hardly blame the car itself when it boiled dry on the outskirts of Bridgetown. It could certainly have chosen far more inconvenient places, she grudgingly admitted. Nevertheless, it took a good ten minutes to obtain some water from the nearest dwelling, and it was already well after twelve-thirty when she finally reached the town centre.

Finding a place to park at that time of day proved difficult. Eventually Tessa left the car in a side street some way above Broad Street, and set off to walk back to Wymans. She was standing on the kerb at one of the main junctions waiting to cross when the familiar white car went past, heading east. Bryn was driving fairly slowly due to the heavy traffic, and he was not alone. Thea's face was turned towards him, her mouth curved in a smile as though he had just said something she found amusing. Then the traffic began accelerating again and they passed from sight, leaving Tessa still standing on the kerb edge with her pipe dreams dispersing about her like smoke on a windy day.

Somehow she made herself start walking again, crossing over the road with a stream of other pedestrians. What was it Bryn had said about taking an unfair advantage? He had done that all right, but she couldn't have made it easier for him. Laughably easy! She wanted to curl up inside when she thought of the way she had gone to him last night, so trustingly eager to believe what he had told her. She paused there. What *had* he told her, when it all boiled down? He had made no promises, no declarations. All he had had to do was hint at the possibility of something growing between them once she had finished with Val. And for what? Because he was determined to get Greenways.

He would have jumped at the excuse to leave her this morning, she thought numbly. He must have been bored to tears. Thea was the kind of woman he was used to being with. Well, let him have her! But he needn't think he was going to get Greenways as well!

The impressive façade that was her goal came into view. Tessa went in at the main entrance and straight up to the first floor, asking an assistant on the way where she could find Mr. Wyman's office. His secretary was expecting her, and directed her through with a smile. A moment later Val was rising from his desk to greet her.

'I'd almost given you up,' he said. 'I was just about to ask Amelia to pop out for a sandwich for me, but now that you're here I'm sure we can find somewhere to have a quick lunch.'

'I'd just as soon have a sandwich myself,' Tessa offered, feeling that any food at all would choke her. 'It's too hot to eat much.' She glanced round the orderly room, wandered over to the window and looked down at the flow of traffic east along Broad Street, then turned back to lean against the sill. 'So this is where you work.'

Val was studying her with a faint anxiety. 'Tessa, you sounded very offhand on the phone. Is something wrong?'

'I was feeling guilty, I suppose,' she improvised quickly. She knew she owed him the truth, but she couldn't bring herself to say it. Not yet, at any rate. 'I'm sorry about last night, Val.'

'It doesn't matter now.' He sounded relieved. 'It just wasn't like you to be difficult.'

Where Val was concerned, Tessa didn't imagine it was. He was usually so agreeable himself that one just went along with him. It occurred to her to wonder if perhaps that very agreeableness was calculated in a way, then she took herself sharply to task for trying to find fault where none existed simply as a sop to her own conscience.

'I'll try not to be again,' she promised, and changed the subject by asking, 'Can we have some coffee with those sandwiches?'

'Of course.' He went at once to dispatch his secretary on her errand.

Tessa drove over to Bathsheba after leaving Val, and sat for a long time watching the surf breaking in flurries of white foam on the pale sands. There were few people in the water. Only the strongest swimmers could combat the currents which swept this Atlantic side of the island.

The reluctance to return home was due, she knew, to a dread of seeing Bryn again. She had been a gullible little fool, and she needed time to compose herself before they did meet. Even now he would be wondering where she had got to; it seemed unlikely that he would guess she had seen him in town. Tessa had no intention of enlightening him on that point either. Let him sort out the details for himself. She only wished she need never set eyes on him again.

She had to go back some time, of course. She arrived about four, glad to find her mother already home.

'You didn't say you were going out,' commented the latter mildly. 'Bryn was on the phone about half an hour ago asking for you. I'd thought you must still be over there up until then.'

'I went down to town to see Val.' Keeping her voice carefully expressionless, she added, 'Did Bryn say what he wanted?'

'No, he didn't. I daresay he'll phone again, or come over, if it's important.' Shirley Wright eyed her daughter thoughtfully. 'He sounded a bit evasive. Everything is all right, isn't it?'

'Of course.' Tessa forced a smile. 'Did you get everything done that you planned?'

The sidetracking was successful enough to keep the conversation flowing until Oliver came flying up the lane from the school bus, and by then her mother appeared to have forgotten about Bryn's call. Almost unrecognizable from the wan little figure of the previous afternoon, the younger Wright offspring lost no time in changing from his school clothes into trunks and sneakers. Ten minutes after arriving home he was vanishing over the rise in the direction of his beloved pool.

Tessa spent the next hour anticipating either a call or a visit from Bryn, but received neither. When Oliver returned for tea he made no mention of having seen anything of him, so Tessa assumed he had gone out again. Only then was she able to relax a little. It was doubtful that he would try getting in touch again this evening, and by tomorrow she would be more in possession of her emotions. What she was going to say to him when she did see him she couldn't begin to work out as yet, which was all the more reason to welcome the reprieve.

'Are you looking forward to moving down to the coast?' she asked her young brother when he was on his way to bed later. 'There'll be a lot more for you to do.'

He considered the question, stifling a yawn. 'Well, there's the sea' he conceded 'and the boat. Uncle Roland says he'll show me how to handle it. I'll miss Greenways, though, an' Bay Marris.' He got into bed, sitting with his knees drawn up to his chest to look at her with some curiosity. 'I heard Mom and Val talking this morning about Greenways. Mom said that if everything worked out the house would be her wedding present. Are you going to marry Val, Tessa?'

'Would you like it if I did?' she parried on a deliberately light note.

The answer came sleepily as he snuggled down beneath the single sheet. 'I don't think he'd be much fun.'

No, thought Tessa on her way out of the room, he probably wouldn't at that. Val was essentially the serious type, and as a married man he might even become more so. It was a depressing outlook, and definitely not for her. She must tell him soon, she acknowledged. The longer she left things as they were the worse it was going to be. Only not before tomorrow night. She was going to need some support to carry her through the ordeal of Bryn's dinner party.

It rained heavily during dinner, leaving the ground refreshed and the night scents sharp and spicy in the clean air. Tessa took her coffee out on the veranda, listening to the deep-throated croaking of frogs from the gully which all but drowned out the normal night sounds. The rain had stopped, but there was a steady drip-drip from the eaves, and the overflowing waterbutt under the fall pipe, creating a rhythmic backing to the symphony.

A car sounded out on the lane, and her heart jerked. Fatalistically she heard it turn into the driveway and stop, heard the slam of a door and footsteps approaching. She didn't move a muscle when Bryn appeared round the corner of the house.

'Waiting for me?' he said from the bottom of the steps. 'I've been expecting you over all afternoon.'

'I didn't get back till late.' Tessa came unsteadily to her feet as he came on up. 'Would you like some coffee? It's freshly made.'

'Thanks, I've not long since had some.' His glance went to the open glass doors behind her. 'Is your mother in?'

'She's in the study sorting through some things.'

'Good, then that gives us time to sort out a few things ourselves.' He leaned against the rail and eyed her consideringly. 'I gather you saw Val?'

She swallowed. 'Yes.'

There was a brief wait, then he said in the same even tones, 'Well, did you tell him or didn't you?'

'No, I didn't.' Up until that moment Tessa had not known how she was going to handle this moment when it came. Now she found the words forming themselves.

'If and when I tell Val I don't want to marry him it's going to be because I've decided it for myself, not because someone else decides it for me.'

The grey eyes narrowed. 'I seem to remember it being a mutual agreement last night – and sleeping on it didn't appear to have affected your feelings on the subject this morning. Why the sudden switch now?'

'Maybe it isn't as sudden as it seems.' Her chin lifted with a certain defiance. 'I may be just a bit of a kid in your opinion, but don't imagine I take everything said to me at face value. The only reason you want me to break with Val is because you don't get this place if I do marry him.'

His jaw had hardened dangerously. 'Is that your considered opinion?'

His anger seemed real enough to give her momentary pause, then the memory of Thea's laughing face in the car swept away all further doubt. 'It's one a few kisses isn't going to alter.' She cast around for some way to make it convincing, and found it. 'You're not the only one capable of putting on an act, Bryn. Like you said, old grudges take a long time dying!'

He made an abrupt movement towards her, checking as Shirley Wright appeared in the open doorway.

'I thought that was your car I heard,' she said pleasantly. 'Sorry I didn't come right out, but I had an armful of Oliver's old manuscripts and couldn't find anywhere to put them down. Have you eaten?'

'An hour ago, thanks.' The lean features were controlled again. 'Did Oliver keep all his original drafts?'

'Along with every bit of correspondence about them. I never knew why. It was just a thing he had.' Her smile held a faint shadow. 'I could never bring myself to do anything about them up until now, but I can hardly take them with me. I know it's sentimental and ridiculous, but the thought of putting a match to them—' she broke off with a half-embarrassed shrug.

'Let me take them with me,' offered Bryn. 'I'll put them in the car now and dispose of them over at Bay Marris.'

'Would you?' She was eager and grateful. 'You probably think I'm being rather silly about the whole thing.'

'No, I think it's perfectly understandable.'

'Thanks. You wouldn't say no to a drink, would you?'

'Not if you're holding a gun to my head.'

Tessa stayed where she was as the two of them went indoors, her nerves slowly settling again. She didn't want to think about what might have happened had her mother not chosen that moment to put in an appearance. She had hit out at Bryn and he had been about to retaliate – that much had been plain from his expression. She hoped he would be content to leave it there. She didn't think she could face another few minutes like the last. And it was all such a waste of time. If she wasn't going to marry Val then Greenways would have to be sold anyway, and Bryn wasn't the type to cut off his nose to spite his face.

So why not let him have it? she thought wearily. She was sick of the whole business. In fact, the sooner she got away from here the better!

Bryn came back to the doorway, pausing there, glass in hand, to view her with cold features.

'Your mother went to stack the rest of the papers,' he said. 'That gives me about five minutes to say what I want to say to you. One should be enough.' His lips twisted at her involuntary movement. 'Don't worry, I'm not going to come near you. I might just do something I'd regret if I did. You need showing—' He cut off what he had been about to say, set his jaw and went on, 'True enough I wanted this place – it was a part of Waldron's original plan for Bay Marris. But if getting one up on me means so much to you then I'll count it right out of my plans from now on. Will that satisfy you?'

Tessa felt too numb to register any particular emotion. 'You said that once before,' she reminded him, 'but you tried again.'

'Sure I did.' His mouth was sardonic. 'I couldn't resist the opportunity. Seems I underestimated you, though. That won't happen again.'

Tessa turned away to lean on the rail and gaze out into the night. 'Why don't you just go away?' she suggested huskily.

'I aim to do just that as soon as your mother lets me have those papers. If it's any consolation, I'll be leaving the island next weekend. Now that I know where I stand I can put the plans already made into effect.'

She refused to move from her position, afraid to let him see her face. She wanted to ask if Thea would be leaving with him, but there was no way of doing that without giving herself away. 'Then you won't be here for the wedding,' she said. 'Mom will be disappointed.'

'But not the maid of honour.' There was a glassy thud as he set his drink down on the rattan table. 'It was nice while it lasted. I should have made more of it.' There was a pause; she could feel his eyes boring into her back. 'You might try using a little more of that acting ability tomorrow night to stop the animosity showing. I'd like the occasion to be free of undercurrents. And don't try wriggling out of it by developing a sudden headache, or similar, because I'll come and damn well fetch you over myself if necessary.'

Tessa had wanted him to go, yet when the stillness behind her told her that he had she felt bereft. She waited where she was until she heard him go out to the car a few moments later, listening to the sound of his departure with an odd sense of detachment. So that was that. Finally and irrevocably.

But it wasn't quite final yet, an inner voice whispered. It wouldn't be over until Bryn had gone from Barbados. Only then could she start to pick up the pieces.

CHAPTER EIGHT

THE morning was hot and hazy after the rain, the distances shimmering against a high blue sky. On a day like this it was good to feel the trade winds against the skin, to see the fresh blowing green of the casuarinas and catch the mingled scents of a dozen or more different species of plant life. It was not a climate for moping in, Tessa acknowledged. It never had been. One only had to listen to Martha singing some old Bajan folk song in the kitchen to appreciate the basic contentment which pervaded the island's people.

Blake Summers' telephone call right after breakfast took her by surprise. It had been days since she had even thought about her old set of friends.

'Don't see much of you these days,' he said. 'Thought you might like to join us in the outboard. We're planning on doing a spot of fishing – maybe get a couple of barracuda.'

The thought of a whole day away from any reminder of the coming evening was more than enough to tempt her. 'Love it,' she said. 'But I'll have to be back by fiveish, Blake.'

'Done!' He sounded mildly triumphant. 'Rob bet me I wouldn't get you to say yes in case Val Wyman didn't approve.' Perhaps fortunately he didn't bother to wait for any comment from her. 'We'll pick you up on the Wharf at ten, by the Da Costa warehouse. You can make it down to town on your own?'

'Yes, of course.'

'Good. See you.' He rang off.

Tessa smiled ruefully as she put down the receiver at her end. Rob obviously believed she had cast them off in favour of new associations. She couldn't blame him in view of her lack of communication this last week. If she were totally truthful she wasn't nearly as enthusiastic about the idea of a day's fishing with the Summers boys as she might once have been. She had outgrown them, she realised. All the same, it would get her out for a few hours.

Her mother gave her a shrewd look when she outlined her plans for the day.

'Aren't you worried that Val might have something to say about you going off like this?' she asked.

Tessa said steadily, 'It isn't really anything to do with Val. He doesn't have any claim on me.'

'He has your promise to think about giving him one.' Her mother shook her head. 'Tessa, you never really had any intention of saying yes to Val, did you?'

It took her a moment to reply. 'It wasn't quite like that. I mean, I liked him a lot – I still do. Only—' Her voice tailed off.

'Only you can't make yourself fall in love with someone to order,' her mother finished for her gently. 'Especially when you're already half-way to being in love with someone else.' She smiled faintly at the jerk of her daughter's bright head. 'I'm not blind, darling. I suspected it when you first told us about Val's proposal last week, but I had to give it a few days to be sure. I'm only sorry it had to be Bryn. I'm very fond of him, but he's hardly the kind of man I would have wanted you to marry. He's too old for you, for one thing – and I don't mean just in years either.' Her voice briskened. 'On the other hand, I wouldn't want you to marry anyone just because you think it might be expected of you. Neither would Roland. So I think you should tell Val as soon as possible.'

'Tonight?'

'If the opportunity arises. Obviously you can't tell him in company.'

'Obviously.' Tessa's smile was wry. 'I only hope it isn't going to spoil things for you and Roland at all.'

'I'm quite sure it isn't. Perhaps it was the speed in which our affairs came to a head that sparked Val off to propose to you at such short notice in the first place.' Rather strangely she added, 'He's a very tidy-minded young man. Anyway, go and enjoy yourself with Rob and Blake for the day. And Tessa,' on a softer note as she started to turn away, 'I know you'll not believe it now but some day you'll meet somebody who will make you forget all about Bryn.'

Tessa was sure she was right, up to a point. She might indeed find someone who would come to mean as much to her as Bryn did, but she could never forget him. They said no woman ever forgot her first love.

She reached Bridgetown at nine-fifty, cutting straight through to Trafalgar Square and round by the Fountain Gardens to cross over the inner basin by the Charles Duncan O'Neale bridge. It was still barely ten when she made it back along Bay Street to the Wharf. She left the car tucked away in a convenient corner behind one of the warehouses, and walked round to the waterfront to look for the familiar little blue and white craft in which she had spent many a happy hour over the past two or three years. If she knew the Summers they'd probably be late anyway. They always were. Tessa had often tried to adjust herself to the Bajan attitude towards time, but never succeeded. Perhaps having spent her formative years in England might have something to do with it. Both Rob and Blake had been born right here in Barbados, like Oliver.

As she had anticipated, there was no sign of the *Sea Bird*, but the yacht moored alongside the Da Costa warehouse was certainly familiar. Eric Varley hailed her from the deck, crossing over to port to look down at her with a jaunty grin.

'Coincidence?' he asked. 'Or did some little bird whisper that I'd returned to roost?'

'I came down to meet some friends to go fishing,' Tessa explained quickly. 'I thought you'd left Barbados for good, Eric.'

An odd expression momentarily chased across his features. 'Any reason why I should?'

'No, of course not. It's just that I remembered Val saying you were heading for the Azores next, and I took it for granted that was where you had gone.' She was floundering without quite knowing why. The remark had been innocent enough, yet Eric seemed to have read some deeper meaning into it. 'Will you be staying longer this time?'

'Only till tonight.' He glanced back along the Wharf. 'Your friends appear to be late. Why not come aboard and have a drink while you're waiting?' The grin flashed again at her hesitation. 'Not so hidebound by convention, are you? We shan't be alone. I carry a crew.'

The crew turned out to be a young Puerto Rican who was in the galley when they went down. He looked at Tessa with frank interest as Eric took her through into the large, sumptuously fitted main cabin. She accepted his invitation to a seat on one of the long banquettes running under the broad, square ports, appraising her surroundings while he poured the iced lime juice she had requested. The bulkheads were panelled in mahogany, with a deep red fitted carpet and dark blue curtains and covers complementing the rich grain. There was a long centre table, at present scattered with charts and papers, and over in one corner a fitted bar fronted in dark blue leather. The door beyond would lead to the sleeping cabins, she surmised.

Eric brought over her drink. 'Not bad, is she? Only took her maiden voyage three months ago. She cost a packet, I can tell you!'

'She's beautiful,' Tessa agreed. 'Did you design her yourself?'

'God, no. I got her from the fellow who did, though.' A smile touched his lips as if at some satisfying memory. 'Found he'd bitten off rather more than he could chew.'

That explained a lot. Tessa had found the rich darkness of the decor somewhat restrained for the flamboyant tastes of the man in front of her. Today he was wearing tight yellow jeans and a knitted cotton shirt in a vivid shade of purple which was open to the waist and held in place by a broad suede belt with a silver clasp like two serpents intertwined. Yet it suited him, she had to admit. Far more than did the Rio. At least he had had the sense to leave that as it was and not try introducing colour here too.

'Tell me what you've been doing with yourself since I left,' he said easily, dropping to a seat alongside her.

She laughed. 'It's only been a week.' That simple statement brought an odd sensation. Only a week, yet she felt years older. 'I had a win at the races on Thursday. I suppose you could call that a high spot.'

'Did Val Wyman take you?' The question was casual.

'We were with his father and my mother. They're going to be married.'

'Really?' He looked interested. 'Nobody mentioned that fact last week.'

'Nobody knew – at least, he hadn't asked her then.'

'And you call a win at the races the only high spot!' He paused a moment before adding lightly, 'I was under the impression that Val had an eye on you in that way too. He could hardly bear to let you out of his sight at that party of theirs.'

Tessa said a shade too quickly, 'We're just good friends.'

'And the other man – Marshall, I think his name was – is he just a friend too?'

She cast him an oblique glance. 'He's our neighbour.'

'Really?' It was obvious that the answer had not told him what he wanted to know. Another brief pause, then he said frankly, 'I've been trying to think where we might have run into one another, but I can't say I remember him from anywhere. Did he happen to mention it to you, by any chance?'

Tessa kept her face carefully expressionless. 'I believe you might have a mutual friend – a Brazilian lady.'

His smile held an element of relief. 'We might have quite a few of those. Is that all he told you?'

'If you mean did he mention her name, no, he didn't. Just that you'd almost broken up her marriage.'

'Ah!' The exclamation was soft with sudden comprehension. 'That one! Trust that little darling to come out of it as the injured party. I suppose she forgot to mention that she kept her husband a pretty close secret until she thought she'd got me well and truly hooked. And she was the one who wanted to do the breaking up.' He shook his head, the smile still hovering. 'I'd naturally be the villain of the piece for running out on her. Guess I just don't believe in coming between husband and wife.'

Tessa stirred restlessly, wishing now that she had denied any knowledge of the affair. Whatever the nature of Eric's feelings on the subject of his association with this woman, guilt quite obviously did not come into it. Well, that was between him and his conscience. It was of no particular interest to her who had told the truth of the matter.

'My friends should be here by now,' she said. 'I ought to go up top and see.'

Eric came to his feet. 'You stay here and finish your drink. Pedro will go and check for you.'

'It's a blue and white outboard,' she called after him. She glanced out of the port nearest to her as she subsided back into her seat, but she was sitting on the starboard side of the boat overlooking the far side of the wharf, with no view aft. It was almost ten-thirty. Even allowing for all eventualities the boys should have arrived by this time. And if they'd had to wait a few minutes for her it wouldn't do them any harm.

Pedro was back almost before Eric had sat down again. There was no boat waiting alongside the quay, he told them in fractured English, but one of the warehousemen had said that such a craft had come in about ten minutes previously and left again almost immediately afterwards.

Tessa knew at once what would have happened. She could have kicked herself for not having thought of it before. Knowing they were late arriving, and knowing she was always pretty well on time herself, they would have simply taken it for granted that she had changed her mind – especially considering Rob's views.

'Guess I did the wrong thing bringing you below for that drink,' Eric commented, not looking in the least apologetic. 'They can't have got far yet. I'll take you out after them.'

'It's not that important, thanks.' Tessa could imagine the reception she would get from the brothers if she accepted the offer. 'I'm not even sure which way they'll be heading.'

'Well, then, come on out for the blow. I was planning a run round the south-east side of the island and now that you're free—'

Tessa's first inclination was to decline politely, then she thought, why not? The other alternative was to return home, and right now she didn't want to be at home. And in spite of what Bryn thought of him, Eric was pleasant enough company. In fact, he was just what she needed to take her out of herself. She looked at him and smiled. 'That sounds tempting, except – well, how long were you thinking of staying out? I have to be back by late afternoon.'

'Good enough. I have an appointment myself at four.' He nodded to the hovering Pedro. 'Tell Vincente to take her out.'

There was a certain sly amusement in the glance the young South American sent Tessa's way, almost as if he knew something she didn't; or was she imagining things? Alone again with Eric in the cabin, she said, 'You carry two crew, then?'

'That's right. Vincente is Italian. He's been with me for years.' He did not add in what capacity. He held out a hand for her empty glass. 'Would you like another of those?'

She shook her head. 'Not for the moment thanks. I've had enough.'

There was a shout overhead, the sound of brisk movement, then the engine sprang to life and they began to move, slipping down past the other vessels at present occupying the Careenage to head for the open sea. Tessa watched the sparkling white foam of their bow wave curling away below as they cut through the glistening sheet of still water, feeling the humming vibration beneath her feet and revelling in the cool draught of circulated air from the vent over the door. the *Rio* had everything.

Eric joined her again as they began to parallel the coast about half a mile out, a freshly mixed Colada in his hand. 'I wouldn't mind settling here myself some time,' he remarked. 'It's one of the few stable places left – politically speaking. Think you'll ever leave it yourself?'

Only a week ago Tessa would have found little difficulty in answering that question; today she hesitated before lifting her shoulders in a noncommittal shrug. 'Who knows? I suppose it depends on what I decide to do with my life.'

'Don't you mean on who you decide to marry?'

She shot him a glance. 'There are other things.'

'For some. You're the type to give your all to the man you fell for.' His tone was light but with an underlying note that came close to regret. 'It's been a long time since I last came across that dewy look. You make me feel even more jaded than I should.'

She said wryly, 'There are times when I wish I was about thirty. Being young isn't all that great.'

'I wouldn't call thirty the gateway to old age,' on a dry note. 'Anyway, don't rush it, it'll come soon enough. Meantime, make the most of what you've got – and you've got plenty, honey!' He laughed at her change of expression. 'Just stating a fact. With that face and that body you could go far. I could think of some who'd give a fortune to have the same natural advantages.'

Tessa didn't care for the drift the conversation was taking. Yet she should have anticipated it. Eric was simply carrying on from where they had left off, and in a manner which probably came as naturally to him as breathing.

'Is it a business appointment you have this afternoon?' she asked pointedly.

'Sort of.' He accepted the change of subject good-humouredly. 'The man I'm meeting should have been here last week, in which case I'd be miles away now. As it is I'm going to be cutting it fine to make—' he seemed to catch himself up there – 'to make my next appointment.' He drained his glass and stood up. 'How about going up top?'

Whatever that next appointment was he was obviously not prepared to divulge any further information. Tessa had the feeling that it might be wisest not to know too much anyway. Recalling what Bryn had already told her of his suspicions concerning her host, she doubted the wisdom of being here with Eric at all, although whatever slightly shady practices he might be involved in, she was fairly certain there was nothing really bad about him. He was an opportunist, that was all.

They had lunch on deck, picking out landmarks as they cruised slowly along the coast with Vincente at the wheel. The Italian was a man in his early forties, with a short, powerful build and a sallow, pockmarked skin. From the brief glance he had directed Tessa's way when she followed Eric on deck earlier she had gathered that he disapproved of her presence on board the *Rio* for some reason of his own. She felt vaguely uncomfortable knowing it, and telling herself that it was no concern of his who his employer invited as a guest did little to relieve that sense of intrusion.

Eric stripped to trunks after they had eaten, and stretched out in the sun. He was going a bit flabby about the middle, Tessa noted dispassionately. He would have a paunch before he was forty if he didn't do something about it. She was wearing a bikini under her blue cotton pants and shirt, but she made no attempt to follow his example. Instead she rested under the awning rigged up over the after deck, ill at ease and wishing she could find an excuse to suggest an early return to Bridgetown.

Yet what was awaiting her when she did get back? There was the whole long evening to be got through, the pain of being so close to Bryn and yet further away from him than she had ever been. And Thea would be there to make matters worse. She would be glad when they had both left Barbados. Perhaps then she would finally be able to accept things as they were.

She had thrown one arm across her eyes to shield them from the reflected glare of the sun on the white-painted superstructure. The first intimation she had of Eric's closeness was when his lips touched hers, lightly at first and then with increasing pressure as her whole body tensed. She pushed fiercely at his chest with the flat of her hands, twisting her head free and sliding out and away from him to sit up with a jerk.

'I didn't come out here with you for that,' she said abruptly.

'No?' He didn't seem particularly put off. His expression was quizzical. 'What did you expect? I never tried to make myself out the avuncular type.'

'I know. I suppose I should have had more sense.' She was more irritated than anything. 'Do you always feel bound to run true to form?'

His grin was disarming. 'Subtlety wastes so much time. Don't you like being kissed, or are you saving it all up for your one true love?'

'I don't care for it being taken for granted, that's all.' She didn't meet his eyes. 'I'd like to go back, if you don't mind.'

'I do. But if that's what you want—' He got up, holding out a hand to help her to her feet. 'Far be it from me to hold you here against your will.'

There were plenty more fish in the sea; he didn't have to say it, she was well aware of it. The irritation faded and she even found herself beginning to smile back, but Eric was no longer looking at her, he was looking beyond her, eyes narrowed into the sun. Following his gaze, she saw a launch coming up fast in their wake, a figure plainly visible at the wheel. Tessa's heart lurched, then steadied again as she recognized the dark head.

'It's Bryn Marshall,' she said.

Eric was the first to move, tossing an order to Vincente in the wheelhouse, then going over to the port side to be ready with a rope as the other vessel drew level. There was a gentle bump as Bryn brought the launch skilfully alongside. Only then did Tessa see the other man standing in the cockpit well ready to take over the wheel while Bryn transferred to the larger craft. The latter came on board lithely, his eyes going first to Tessa.

'You all right?' he clipped.

'Doesn't she look all right?' Eric sounded more amused than anything else. 'What are you, the family guard dog?'

There was no visible change in Bryn's expression, no signalling of intention, just a blur of movement as he spun on his heel and sent the other sprawling on his back with a powerful right to the jaw. Voice low but carrying, he said over his shoulder, 'Tessa, get aboard the launch.'

Vincente had left the wheel and was moving aft, looking mean and suddenly dangerous. Only when his employer held up a hand and shook his head did he pause, and then with reluctance. Eric made no attempt to get to his feet, propping himself up on one elbow to ruefully finger his jaw and eye his adversary.

'Guess I had that coming,' he said. 'Didn't realise I was treading on any toes.'

Bryn didn't bother to reply, nor did he spare a glance in the direction of the younger man who had appeared in the hatchway to see what the commotion was about. Tessa found her arm grasped none too gently, and was over the side and standing in the launch without being any too sure of exactly how she had got there. There was a brief exchange of words on board the *Rio*, then Bryn was joining her and they were pulling away in a great curve back in the direction of Bridgetown.

Tessa looked into the set features and felt the mental paralysis of the last few minutes abruptly disperse. There were a dozen questions she wanted to ask, but only one she could bring herself to voice.

'How did you know where I was?'

'One of the boys you were supposed to be meeting telephoned to find out what had happened to you.' His tone was hard. 'Your mother contacted me because she was afraid you might have had an accident on the way down to town. I followed your route down to the Wharf and found out that you'd been seen boarding the *Rio*, so I hired this and came after you.' He made a small movement towards her, as though he would have liked to take hold of her and shake her, then visibly got a hold on himself. 'Didn't anything of what I told you about Eric Varley make any impression?'

She said slowly, 'I only intended to have a quick drink with him while I was waiting for Blake and Rob. When

Pedro said they'd come in and gone out while I was on board the *Rio*, Eric suggested a trip round the coast as a kind of compensation. That's all there was to it.'

'On your part, maybe. Varley's type does nothing without a motive. You're not going to tell me he didn't try to make love to you?'

Tessa's chin jutted suddenly. 'So he did, but he was perfectly willing to bring me back when I asked him. You had no right to come barging in like some – some Victorian brother!'

Grey eyes sparked. 'I had every right! Apart from anything else, do you think I'd risk having you involved in whatever it is that brought friend Varley back to Barbados? There's every chance that the authorities already know all about his activities in these waters, and if they don't they damn well should!'

'What activities?' with rather less aggression.

'I don't know all the details, just enough to get a good idea of his racket.' He paused, glancing aft in the direction of the fast dwindling white yacht. 'Varley makes his living arranging for others to avoid paying the premium on overseas investments, among other things. The charge would probably be "conspiracy to defraud". And that's as much as you need to know.'

It was as much as she wanted to know. It explained the look on Eric's face when he had spotted the launch chasing after them. He must have believed it was the long arm of the law catching up with him. She felt nothing but relief at being out of it. Let Eric take care of himself. What did trouble her was the fact that Bryn had been forced into coming after her this way. Though only for her mother's sake, she reminded herself numbly.

'I suppose I should thank you for rescuing me,' she said with a faint tilt of her head. 'It was decent of you to go to so much trouble.'

He looked at her for a long hard moment, the expression in his eyes bringing a tinge of colour to her cheeks. 'Don't push your luck too far,' he said. 'The way I feel I could wring your neck!' He turned abruptly away to join the man at the wheel leaving Tessa to contemplate sea and sky alone.

They made it back to Bridgetown inside half an hour. Bryn paid off the boatman, then took Tessa in near silence round to where he had left his car.

'I came down in the Morris,' she reminded him when he opened the passenger door.

'I know.' He made no move to amend his action. 'You can collect it later. I don't trust you to go straight home under your own steam.'

There was no point in arguing about it. Tessa was beyond wanting to argue about anything any more. She slid into the seat, sitting quietly while Bryn went round to get behind the wheel. In roughly half an hour he would deposit her at Greenways, and that would be that. This was the last time they would ever be alone together; he would take care to see that it was. Some time soon that knowledge was going to hit and hurt, but for the moment she felt nothing in particular. The sun dazzled her eyes as they left the shelter of the warehouse and she put up a hand to shade them, seeing the blue sheen of the water through a kind of mist. She blinked and it cleared, bringing the colourful waterfront scene into focus with a sharpness that was almost too intense.

They were less than half-way home when the rear offside tyre blew out. Cursing under his breath, Bryn brought the car to a slightly skewed halt at the side of the road and switched off before getting out to look at the flat.

'Looks like a piece of glass went through it,' he announced, coming back to get his keys to open the boot. 'I'll have to change the wheel.'

Tessa got out herself as he busied himself with the jack, easing the material of her shirt away from the centre of her back where it clung damply. 'Do you want any help?'

He shook his head without looking up from his task. 'Nothing much you can do. It shouldn't take long.'

There was a clear view from where she stood over the cane fields and down across the belt of green to the white strand of beach. Looking back towards the town she would see the *Rio* standing out beyond Needham's Point. Whatever Eric's faults she couldn't find it in herself to condemn him out of hand. He probably didn't even see what he was doing as anything more than a dodge – something like an income tax fiddle, perhaps. Tessa was hazy about the ins and outs of it, but didn't see all that much difference herself on the face of it. One thing was certain, he would have calculated the risks. Ten to one he would be able to wriggle off the hook if he were caught.

It was no use, she acknowledged. She could stand here pretending an interest in Eric Varley's future, but that was all it was, a pretence; one way of keeping her mind off the man working on the car behind her. She stuck her hands deep into the pockets of her jeans and gazed fixedly out to sea. Loving Bryn was something she was going to have to get over. It would take time, and it wasn't going to be easy, but at least she wouldn't have to go through the ordeal of seeing him constantly. This next week was going to be the most difficult part. Once that was over she would come to some decision over her own future. Maybe she would be better away from Barbados for a spell, particularly as the relationship between her and Val was bound to be awkward for a time. She could go to England; they had some relatives still in business over there. It was something to think about.

She steeled herself to turn round casually when Bryn finally announced the job completed. He was standing by the open boot wiping his hands on a rag, the knees of his white cotton slacks dusty where he had knelt to fix on the spare wheel. Tessa went and got back into her seat. She heard the clang as he shut the boot lid and felt the springs give, then he was getting in beside her, sliding the key into the ignition and switching on. The engine sprang to life, ran for a brief moment, and then abruptly cut out again as he turned off with a sudden savage movement.

'I can't take any more of this,' he said roughly. 'If we have to start again from scratch, then we'll do it, but I'm not going to believe you felt nothing at all when I kissed you yesterday. It was real for both of us I'll swear to that. Tessa—' He turned to look at her, saw the stunned blue eyes and stopped right there, his own expression altering. For a moment neither moved, then he reached out and pulled her over into his arms, finding her mouth with an urgency which jerked her out of her stupor in a way nothing else could have done. There were questions to be asked, and to be answered, but for now they could wait. For Tessa all that mattered at present was the feel of Bryn's arms about her, of his lips on hers, of the warmth and joy spreading through her like sunlight pushing back the shadows. No holding back this time. He was kissing her as a man would kiss the woman he loved and wanted beyond all others, and she was responding in kind, without reticence, without fear, without thought of anything other than the desperate need to be close to him.

It was several minutes before the first urgency of discovery abated enough to allow rational thought to return, and even then Bryn would not let her go, holding her to him with his face against her hair. '*Why*, Tessa?' he murmured. 'If you felt like this, why all that guff last night? Have you any idea what I've been going through this last twenty-four hours?'

'About the same as I have, I expect.' Her voice was shaky. She tried to be adult about it, to state her case calmly and unemotionally and wait for his explanation with an open mind. 'I saw you with Thea yesterday. I'd gone into town to meet Val to tell him I couldn't marry him, and you passed me on the corner of Broad Street and Sheppherd Street. You were both laughing, and I wanted to die.' She had meant the last to sound wryly humorous, but somehow it came out with a tremulousness which made her hurry on. 'I thought you'd been playing with me, taking advantage of how I felt to get me to finish with Val so that you could have Greenways.'

'Damn Greenways,' he said forcibly. 'If I hadn't been so quick with that offer we might have got things straightened out between us a lot sooner.' He held her a little away from him, his hand curving her neck, his gaze direct. 'True, that phone call was from Thea, reminding me I was supposed to be picking her up to take her to lunch with some folk out on the east coast. I could have told you about it, but I thought it was one of those matters best left alone. I intended to keep the luncheon arrangement, then make it plain to Thea that I'd be otherwise engaged from then on. If I looked particularly happy it was because I was thinking about us. All right?'

'Yes,' she said huskily. It was so simple when told that way, and she had let that one incident put her through the worst twenty-four hours of her whole life. 'I should have told you I'd seen you, I realize that now. It would have saved such a lot of misunderstanding.'

'Learning to trust someone isn't always that easy. I might have jumped to the same conclusions had the positions been reversed.' Bryn was smiling again. 'We'll have to make a pact that any future doubts will be brought out into the open for discussion before judgment is reached.' His hand still holding her nape was possessive. 'Tessa, you'll have to marry me soon. I've waited five years for this moment, and that's long enough for any man.' Voice soft, he added, 'How do you feel?'

'Trembly,' she admitted, not attempting to conceal the way his touch affected her. She turned her face into his hand and rubbed her cheek against the palm, kissed his fingertips and looked at him with softly luminous eyes. 'If this is a dream I don't ever want to wake up, so don't pinch me!'

'It's no dream, though I'm feeling a bit spellbound myself.' The strong lines of his face were relaxed in a manner she had never hoped to see. 'I love you, little Tess. More than I thought it possible to love anyone. I'm not sure what I expected to find when I came back to Barbados. All I did know was that for five years you'd made it impossible for me to think seriously of any other woman. And I was almost too late, wasn't I? By this time next year you might have been married to Val Wyman.'

'No, not Val.' She was sure of that. 'The only reason I got involved with him in that sense was because it was the only way I had left of hiding my feelings for you.' Her laugh was uneven. 'I spent five years pretending to hate you – and believing it too – but that only worked when you weren't here in person. I'm sorry for all I've said and done this last couple of weeks. You see, I wanted to go on hating you, and when I couldn't I wanted to hurt you instead, in whatever way I could manage. Greenways isn't really all that important to me. It was simply a ready-made opportunity to pay you back for all the unhappiness you caused me.'

'What a tangle!' Bryn sounded rueful. 'Tess, what I told you last night – or was it the night before; I've lost track – anyway, it was perfectly true. I found myself getting too fond of a fourteen-year-old girl and I had to have a defence. If I hurt you I'm sorry too, but there was no other way.'

'I know that now. You couldn't be sure your own feelings would last until I'd grown up, never mind mine.' She paused, hating herself for asking but unable to just leave it either. 'Bryn, did you know Thea for long before you came out here? Closely, I mean.'

'I know what you mean.' His tone was steady. 'I was introduced to her at a party a couple of weeks before leaving New York, and we went to the theatre a couple of times. Until we met up on the plane I'd no notion that she even knew anyone in Barbados. Naturally I was asked over to the de Sousas' as soon as she told them she knew me, and it was a bit difficult then to correct the general assumption that she and I were rather more than just acquaintances.' He shrugged lightly. 'I can't say I objected to her company on occasion; it kept me from getting too hasty over you. On the other hand, I wasn't about to make love to another woman with you only a few miles away like a beacon on the hill.' He traced the line of her mouth with a finger and she could sense the desire in him, but also the restraint. 'I wanted, badly, to make love to you, the night you shoved me in the pool – after I'd got through wanting to wallop you black and blue, that is.' The last on a note of humour. 'You'd tantalized me half out of my mind earlier on, then I come back to that! Could you blame me for getting mad enough to put the fear of God into you?'

'Not really.' Laughing with him, she put her head down to his shoulder. 'Under the circumstances I think you showed remarkable control.' She was silent for a moment, conscious of the tingling delight of having the right to be close to him like this. 'My mother thinks you're too old for me,' she said. 'Isn't that silly?'

'Not so very. She's probably got a point,' he said dispassionately. 'But we're not going to let it make any difference because it happens to have worked out that way. We'll just have to convince her that it will work for us, even if not for others.' His tone altered a little. 'Tessa, you're going to hate leaving Barbados, but I can't see my way to staying on indefinitely. There's a job coming up in the Argentine in a few weeks. I'm more or less committed to taking it on. Do you think you could be ready to marry me inside the month?'

'Yes,' she said without hesitation. 'We can make it the week after Mom's wedding, if you like. That will really make things hum!' She lifted her head and looked at him steadily. 'And you're right about me not wanting to leave the island. It's been my home for so long, and I don't think there can be any other place quite like it. But I'd still rather be anywhere in the world with you than here without you, Bryn. We'll be able to come back; it will always be here.' Her mouth curved shyly. 'We'll be able to bring our children for holidays with their grandmother.'

He laughed. 'That's getting a bit far ahead. I'll want you to myself for a while first. Quite a long while,' he added firmly, pulling her close again. 'I didn't wait five years to share you with anyone too soon.'

Best Seller Romances

Romances you have loved

Mills & Boon Best Seller Romances are the love stories that have proved particularly popular with our readers. They really are "back by popular demand." These are the six titles to look out for this month.

A LYON'S SHARE
by Janet Dailey

Joan Somers had loved her boss, Brandt Lyon, ever since she had come to work for him three years ago. Now, at last, he seemed to be taking an interest in her — but her delight was tinged with a bittersweet uncertainty; for how could she take him seriously when his delightful blonde girl-friend Angela was so clearly still the woman in possession?

BOSS OF BALI CREEK
by Anne Hampson

In marrying Jack, Lorna had followed the dictates of her conscience and not her heart — and had lost the man she loved in the process. Now she was free, and had met Wade again — but he had made it quite clear that he was no longer interested...

Mills & Boon

TO PLAY WITH FIRE
by Flora Kidd

...ry was sure that she loved Magnus — so sure that she gladly ...ok a job on the Caribbean island of Airouna, just to be near ...n. So why was she so attracted to Denzil Hallam, who was ...outed to be the most dangerous man on the island.

FLOWER OF THE DESERT
by Roberta Leigh

...orking in Persia, Fleur had come to like and admire Persian ...ays — but she could never accept their attitude to women as ...ere chattels who should be content to marry and then be ...edient to their husbands in all things. So she had better not fall ...love with a Persian — least of all the attractive Karim Khan. ...t that was easier said than done...

THE ARROGANT DUKE
by Anne Mather

...liet had run away from a domineering father — but her ...uation was hardly improved when she realized that not only ...s her new employer, the Duque Felipe Ricardo de Castro, ...en more domineering, but that she had fallen hopelessly in ...ve with him.

SUGAR CANE HARVEST
by Kay Thorpe

...ssa's carefree existence in her Caribbean home was threatened ...the news that Bryn Marshall was coming back. Their ...ationship had always been uneasy, and she held out no hope ...at now it might be happier. For he seemed no more interested ...her now than he had all those years ago...

the rose of romance

Best Seller Romances

Next month's best loved romances

Mills & Boon Best Seller Romances are the love stories that have proved particularly popular with our readers. These are the titles to look out for next month.

SIX WHITE HORSES Janet Dailey
A MAN TO TAME Rachel Lindsay
DEVIL IN VELVET Anne Mather
NEVER GO BACK Margaret Pargeter
SWEET SUNDOWN Margaret Way
THAT MAN BRYCE Mary Wibberley

Buy them from your usual paperback stockist, or write to: Mills & Boon Reader Service, P.O. Box 236, Thornton Rd, Croydon, Surrey CR9 3RU, England. Readers in South Africa-write to: Mills & Boon Reader Service of Southern Africa, Private Bag X3010, Randburg, 2125.

Mills & Boon
the rose of romance

The romantic gift for Christmas

First time in paperback, four superb romances by favourite authors, in an attractive special gift pack. A superb present to give. And to receive.

United Kingdom £3.80
Publication 14th October 1983

Darkness of the Heart
Charlotte Lamb

Lost in Summer Madness
Carole Mortimer

Virtuous Lady
Madeleine Ker

Man-Hater
Penny Jordan

Look for this gift pack where you buy Mills & Boon romances

Mills & Boon.
The rose of romance.

FREE - an exclusive Anne Mather title, MELTING FIRE

At Mills & Boon we value very highly the opinion of our readers. What you tell us about what you like in romantic reading is important to us.

So if you will tell us which Mills & Boon romance you have most enjoyed reading lately, we will send you a copy of MELTING FIRE by Anne Mather – absolutely FREE.

There are no snags, no hidden charges. It's absolutely FREE.

Just send us your answer to our question, and help us to bring you the best in romantic reading.

CLAIM YOUR FREE BOOK NOW
Simply fill in details below, cut out and post to: Mills & Boon Reader Service, FREEPOST, P.O. Box 236, Croydon, Surrey CR9 9EL.

The Mills & Boon story I have most enjoyed during the past 6 months is:

TITLE _____
AUTHOR _____
BLOCK LETTERS, PLEASE
NAME (Mrs/Miss) _____ EP4
ADDRESS _____
_____ POST CODE _____

Offer restricted to ONE Free Book a year per household. Applies only in U.K. and Eire.
CUT OUT AND POST TODAY – NO STAMP NEEDED.

Mills & Boon
the rose of romance